Was it reasonable to feel so angry?

Prunella was still in a turmoil of mixed feelings over Rourke's identity. Was it foolish to hope that there was some decent excuse for his deception? Was it dangerous to be plotting his come-uppance if no excuse was forthcoming? With a sigh she abandoned these questions as unanswerable.

It's my own fault for seeing him as an instant friend, she told herself. And for letting yourself find him attractive, a deeper voice said.

Dear Reader

We're travelling the world this month! Angela Devine bases her story in Sydney, and, as well as being a marvellous romance, it makes a good case for donating blood. Frances Crowne takes us to Germany and troubled teenagers, while Lilian Darcy explores an unusual area of Canada. Closer to home, there is another excellent story from Caroline Anderson—you will adore Ross! Enjoy. . .

The Editor

Lilian Darcy is Australian, but on her marriage made her home in America. She writes for theatre, film and television, as well as romantic fiction, and she likes winter sports, music, travel and the study of languages. Hospital volunteer work and friends in the medical profession provide the research background for her novels; she enjoys being able to create realistic modern stories, believable characters, and a romance that will stand the test of time.

Recent titles by the same author:

THE CHALLENGE OF DR BLAKE
A PRACTICAL MARRIAGE

CLOSER TO A STRANGER

BY

LILIAN DARCY

MILLS & BOON LIMITED
ETON HOUSE   18–24 PARADISE ROAD
RICHMOND   SURREY   TW9 1SR

*First published in Great Britain 1992
by Mills & Boon Limited*

© Lilian Darcy 1992

*Australian copyright 1992
Philippine copyright 1992
This edition 1992*

ISBN 0 263 77747 2

*Set in 10 on 11 pt Linotron Baskerville
03-9206-58995*

*Typeset in Great Britain by Centracet, Cambridge
Made and printed in Great Britain*

CHAPTER ONE

THE dog was definitely in pain. From a distance its cries could have been a half-grown puppy's yelps of excitement, and its jerky movements those of an over-enthusiastic young hunter closing in on its quarry, but now that Prunella Murdoch found herself only twenty yards from the animal. . .

'Steady on, fella. . .You're stuck, aren't you, you silly wee thing?' she said, pitching her musical Scottish-accented voice at a low, soothing level. She was in the lee of the cliff now and the voice of the wind was much less in competition with her own than it had been on the open beach. 'Steady on, now, wee lad, I'm coming.'

The animal took no notice. It was becoming more frantic now, its gangling gold-tan limbs jerking and its cries of distress rising to piercing howls. Prunella repeated her words more loudly. The wind did gust here at intervals, in spite of the cliff's protection. As she scrambled over a jagged ridge of rock and could at last see the dog clearly a strand of long blonde hair blew across her mouth and a chill breath of air found bare flesh beneath the loose cowl neck of her Wedgwood-blue pullover.

'I'm here, fella.' she said, ignoring physical discomfort. 'It's all right—you'll be free in a jiffy, I promise.'

The problem was clear now. As the dog became aware of her presence his howls ebbed to a whimper and he stopped the vain struggling of his long limbs. One front paw was wedged in a narrow crevice of steel-grey rock and had been trapped there by a triangular sea-worn stone that had fallen in on top. He must have dislodged the rock himself while sniffing about in these sea-tanged cliffs, and each time he tried to pull free the rock was jiggled into a tighter and tighter fit, pressing down on the paw.

The light gold fur was crimson-stained now in places. His body was twisted at an awkward angle too, and Prunella wondered if the leg was broken as well. Without stopping to think any further, she clambered over the remaining rock obstacles and bent towards the animal. By leaning over him like this she could reach down to the imprisoning rock and——

'Stop!' The voice behind her left shoulder cracked like a gunshot and had her half out of her skin, with her heart poised in mid-beat.

She turned on a gasp of sound and then lost her balance on the jagged sea-worn rocks. The man behind her strode forward, finding his footing on the rocks as if he had been crossing a carpeted floor. Long fingers thrust towards her and gripped her arm in time to save her from an unpleasant fall.

'Didn't mean to startle you,' the stranger said.

Prunella could only gulp and gasp as she found herself safe on a minute plain of coarse sand between two toothed spines of dark rock. The stranger did not wait for a response. His attention was already on the distressed dog, and when he spoke to her again it was over his shoulder.

'Dogs can turn on people when they're in pain,' he said roughly. 'They don't always know when someone's trying to help. I'll get him free.'

'Go ahead, then,' Prunella managed. Broad-shouldered, long-limbed. . . If he felt confident that the dog wouldn't turn on him she wasn't going to argue. She stood back, watching and listening.

'Easy now, fella. . .' He was talking in the same soothing tones that she had used, but his accent wasn't

Scottish like her own. Instead, she recognised the distinctive vowels of a native Newfoundlander.

It was an accent that had taken her by surprise when she had first arrived here in St Anthony, at the northern tip of the huge, wild island that was Canada's easternmost province. She had expected the local people to have a standard Canadian drawl, and the sounds that were a mixture of Cornish, Devon and Irish served to remind her that Newfoundland had only become part of Canada in 1949. The accent sounded quite familiar now, however, and it was difficult at times to realise that she had only been in St Anthony for a little over two weeks. 'That's right,' the stranger was saying. 'I'm taking this rock off your paw and then we'll see what's what.'

He had straddled the crevice with his long legs and was bracing them as he bent his back and wrestled the wedged rock out of the crack with both hands. Prunella saw now that it was bigger than she had thought, and that her own small, slim-fingered hands would have been useless. With a grating sound the rock came free. The stranger threw it aside, then raised his head and addressed Prunella.

'I'll need you now,' he said briefly. With an easy yet careful bound he was down beside the dog, then he crouched so that he was almost on top of the animal, and held its muzzle firmly but not cruelly between his hands. 'You'll have to free the paw,' the man said. 'He can't bite either of us now.'

'All right, but how?' Prunella replied, coming closer. The stranger's energetic confidence had shaken her own.

'Whatever looks best. I can't gauge it,' he said. He was speaking through clenched teeth and she realised that it wasn't easy for him to keep a strong hold on the whimpering dog without causing it further pain.

'Yes, sorry, I'll try my best,' she breathed quickly.

A moment later she was beside the injured animal and

reaching into the crevice towards the wedged paw. Now she found that her small hand was an advantage. The stranger's fingers, although long and slender, would never have been able to manoeuvre their way into this crack.

'His paw's twisted,' she said as soon as she had felt it. It was different in construction from a human hand and forearm, of course, but her nursing training still came in handy.

'Which way?'

'Outwards,' she answered. 'And you see if I try to pull——'

'I know,' he cut her off. 'It'll put too much twist and strain on the joint. Wait, I should be able to lift him.' His voice strained as he bent himself to the task.

The dog was young, but it was large, a mongrel mixture of Labrador, Great Dane and goodness knew what. The stranger managed to turn the creature so that he was on his side, and this meant that, when Prunella twisted the injured paw and worked it free, the leg was brought into comfortable alignment again. At last the animal lay, its whimpering subsiding, on a platform of near-flat rock. His rescuer was panting lightly but had not stopped to rest, and Prunella saw that he had taken a handkerchief from his pocket and was getting ready to bind the bleeding paw.

'Got any tissues?' he asked her without looking up.

'Yes, a hanky, actually, and it's clean. Wait a minute.' She took the square of plain blue cotton and scrambled down to where the waves broke over the rocks. There was a little pool where she could wet the handkerchief. . .

But she had misjudged the waves, and as she sopped the hanky in the pool she was drenched in a breathtakingly cold splash of salt water. Stumbling back to the man and the dog, she felt like an incompetent fool, but when the stranger took the wet square of cloth from her hand without comment she decided with relief that he hadn't seen her drenching.

Carefully he sponged the blood away from the badly-cut paw. 'This salt water will sting, but it can't be helped,' he said.

'Are you a vet?' Prunella asked impulsively. His touch seemed so gentle, and very professional.

He answered with a bark of laughter. 'A vet? No! Not much call for them around here.'

'No, I suppose not,' she answered meekly, feeling a little foolish. As a nurse, she felt that she should be the one dressing the wound, but he had taken charge with such assurance and so successfully that it would be clumsy and insulting if she made a point about her professional status.

There was nothing to do, in that case, except watch. Since he *wasn't* a vet, the man was probably a fisherman. Most of the local people were. Somewhere further along the shore he might have a boat of his own, or perhaps he worked for one of the big offshore fisheries. He was certainly built strongly enough for such physical work, and his face had the healthy and slightly weathered look of someone who spent a lot of time outdoors in harsh conditions. His black hair was as windswept as her own straight blonde tresses must be, and his blue-green eyes, narrowed like a wolf's against the onshore breeze, reflected the colours of the sea itself. He wore a pair of rather workworn jeans, toped by a thick hand-knitted Aran sweater of a navy blue so dark that it was almost black.

'There,' he said as he finished tying the makeshift bandage, 'he should be able to walk now. I'll take him into town and see if I can find out who he belongs to.'

The dog was quiescent, responding with tiny yelps to the caresses of the man who had tended his injury. Prunella reached down and touched the golden-tan fur as well. It was surprisingly soft. The animal was still just a puppy. 'You don't think he could be a stray?'

'No, he's too well fed for that,' he said. The words were spoken absently, and a second later he had peeled the navy pullover over his head and was holding it out to her. 'Here, you can't stay in that wet garment in this wind.'

So he *had* noticed her drenching after all! She was embarrassed, but was having a hard time suppressing the chatter of her teeth by this time and could only give a meek thanks and accept his offer. He took the Wedgwood-blue pullover from her as soon as she removed it and managed to squeeze quite a bit of water from it, turning away from her to do so. Prunella was relieved. At least he had spared himself the sight of her oldest blouse!

The thick, warm weight of the Aran-knit enveloped her. It was far too large, but somehow that felt rather nice, and the very faint aura of masculine perfume that emanated from it was nice too.

But the owner of the garment was still eyeing her critically. 'We'll put Rover here in my car and I'll get you some tea—you need a hot drink. I didn't see another car. You must have walked here from town.'

This last sentence was spoken rather accusingly, and Prunella felt constrained to explain herself. 'I. . . It's my day off,' she said. 'I came along the coves and headlands. I'm new in St Anthony, a nurse at Charles S Curtis. . .at the hospital, and I didn't have anything else to do. . .' And then, conscious that this sounded a little pathetic 'And anyway, I like walking and exploring.'

'Clearly,' he answered. 'But I'll drive you back to town. It seems to be my day for rescuing creatures on the beach.'

'I don't need rescuing, thank you, Mr. . .?'

'Call me Rourke.'

'Mr Rourke.'

'No, not *Mr* Rourke. Just Rourke, thanks. As to the question of your rescue, *I* wouldn't fancy that long walk back to town with the wind biting through my wet pullover.'

'Yes I'm sorry, it's very kind of you to——'

'I wasn't fishing for thanks. . .'

'Well, I'm thanking you anyway,' she said firmly, uneasy about the twists and turns this conversation was taking. 'Rourke.' Rourke who? And was it wise to accept a lift from a stranger even in a place as small and isolated as St Anthony, where everyone knew everybody? Reason told her that she had little choice, having already accepted his pullover, and then she saw his hand touch the injured animal's golden head gently once again, and was reassured. His concern for the dog was genuine, and she had no reason to think that his attitude towards herself was any different.

'My car's just over the rise,' Rourke said. 'Let's see if our friend Rover will follow.'

He clicked his tongue and set off, and both Prunella and the dog—'Rover', as Rourke had facetiously christened it—began to follow gamely after him.

Over the rise, Prunella saw not just a car but a half-finished house as well, and the two things clearly belonged together. 'You're going to be living quite a distance from town,' she said impulsively, then wished she hadn't spoken. The matter was none of her business.

Fortunately he didn't seem to take the comment amiss, but replied on a shrug, 'I like it out here. St Anthony's getting too tame for me, and too crowded. I want an uninterrupted view of the sea.'

'Yes, I love the sea, too, especially when it *isn't* tame.'

And it was this most innocuous of observations that he objected to. 'You "love the sea!" If I had a dollar for every time someone's said that to me. . .' The words exploded on a strong note of derision, and Prunella blinked nervously.

'Well, I suppose a lot of people *do* love it,' she answered him feebly. He was striding the last few yards to the car, and she had a struggle to keep up. Rover was doing better on three legs.

'Yes,' Rourke was saying, 'the way people love lions and panthers—how adorable, just like great big kittens! The sea's too damned dangerous for that sort of sentiment, especially around here. That's why in the past everyone clustered their houses around the harbour, so that the women could count the fishing boats limping in after a storm. . .'

'If you feel so strongly about it. . .!' Prunella began to retort.

They reached the car at that moment, and abruptly he turned to her. 'Am I sounding illogical?' Now, surprisingly, there was a sardonic grin on his windroughened face.

'Yes!' Prunella said, startled into frankness.

'OK,' he acknowledged, 'I won't deny it. I was too sharp a minute ago, but my family has been on this island for several generations. So many of them have lost their lives at sea. There's salt water in our blood, and that's a dangerous mix of fluids. You're a stranger. You've got green eyes, like me, but mine are sea-green. Yours. . .they're a lovely jade, but they're not seagoing eyes. Don't imagine that you'll start to understand the Newfoundlander temperament in a matter of a few weeks.'

'I wouldn't dream of it!' Prunella exclaimed with energy, although inwardly a little disconcerted at his keen study of her eyes. His had been quite mesmerising as they had looked into her own. She went on, 'I never expect to "understand" an individual personality after a few weeks, let alone a regional temperament—if such a thing really exists.'

'You don't think it does?' he challenged.

'Perhaps. . .Let's just say that I think personal character usually overrides it.'

'Hmm.' He shrugged and turned away from her, as if dismissing the theory as something he was reluctant to dwell on. 'Let's get going, shall we?' He glanced at a square-faced wrist-watch and frowned, then added, 'Wait, though—I promised you tea, didn't I? Would you like a cup? And some cake? I have a Thermos, so it won't take long.'

'Oh! Cake as well!' The offer took her by surprise. 'Actually. . .But you——'

'I was spending the afternoon out here working on the house. Brought some provisions and never got round to having them. There are two mugs, and enough cake to share.'

'It would be nice,' Prunella admitted. The sharp twin tastes of thirst and hunger were suddenly in her mouth, and she knew that the evening meal at the hospital dining-room would be at least two hours away.

'I'll see if I can get Rover into the back of the car, then, shall I? If he won't lie down happily. . .'

'Then we should go straight away,' she finished on a nod. 'Of course.'

Absurdly she felt quite disappointed at the prospect of this possibility, and she had to admit to herself—yes, and why not, after all?—that this man Rourke attracted her. Or was that too strong a word, and too specifically physical? It wasn't just the powerful build and hypnotic eyes. He intrigued her—that was better. And on top of this there was the raw fact that she was horribly lonely here in St Anthony.

She stood back while Rourke opened the rear door of his four-wheel-drive vehicle, spread an old overcoat on the seat and half coaxed, half lifted the dog inside. The animal was young enough to give his trust easily, and lay down immediately, his golden fur a contrast to the brown coat and dark grey upholstery of the vehicle. He whimpered a little, however, when Rourke tried to shut the door, so it was left open.

'Now for that tea.'

'I'm looking forward to it more every minute,' Prunella said, allowing not only her thirst for hot liquid but also her thirst for human companionship to colour her tone.

'Like to see over the house as well?' was Rourke's relaxed reply, and again she nodded agreement. It seemed ironic that this little cove, isolated even by St Anthony's standards, should be the place to provide her with the glimmerings of companionship.

'We'll sit by the fireplace, shall we?' Rourke suggested, taking a canvas backpack from the front passenger-seat of the vehicle.

'Fireplace?'

'In the house. No fire lit there yet, of course, but it seems appropriate somehow.'

He led the way inside the stone cottage. Wall, roof and floor were in place, but no doors or windows as yet. Plastic sheeting roughly tacked to window-frames and doorways provided protection against weather-staining on the new floorboards, and the air was spiced with the smell of newly cut wood. It wasn't a large house—two bedrooms, as far as she could judge, but one wooden wall seemed to allow for the possibility of later additions.

By the stone fireplace there were two canvas camp chairs. Two mugs, two slices of cake. . .Prunella wondered suddenly if he had been expecting someone else to join him this afternoon. She remembered the way he had glanced at his watch earlier, and how he had made an explanation about the Thermos, as if he was self-conscious about it somehow. If he *was* expecting someone he had clearly decided that he had been stood up, so perhaps the need for companionship wasn't only on her side.

There was something very cosy about sitting in this unfinished house on the simple chairs. Idly Prunella began to furnish the place in her mind, putting a red-toned Persian carpet on the polished wood floor and interesting china in a corner cabinet, painting the half-finished kitchen cupboards cream with China-blue edging, and tiling the kitchen floor with big, plain matt tiles. As she sipped her tea in silence—it was refreshing but very, very strong—she felt for the first time that it might be possible to forgive Emma for the fact that she was here. . .

It was Emma's idea to apply for the nursing vacancies advertised in February's nursing journal.

'I *have* to get away from Inverness,' she said, as if the very name of the town were mud. 'Everything reminds me of Douglas. . . It's stupid, but there it is. Perhaps on the other side of the world. . .'

Douglas had broken off his engagement to flamboyant Emma in the midst of a fiery argument—by no means their first such scene, and Prunella had always thought privately that they seemed to enjoy these tantrums almost as much as they enjoyed the making up afterwards, but this time the break-up had a greater air of finality.

'If you applied as well, Prunella. . .'

'Me?'

'Yes!' Emma suddenly became as authoritative as a newspaper advice columnist. She might, in fact, have made a very good one. 'You need the change as much as I do, my lass. You're extremely attractive, and yet you're so shy and timid that——'

'I'm not shy,' Prunella retorted, stung, 'let alone timid!'

'All right, but you don't make friends easily, certainly not men friends, anyway—boyfriends.'

This was true. On another occasion Emma had also told Prunella the reason for these drawbacks in her personality. Having done the same psychology courses as part of her nursing training, Prunella knew that Emma's analysis was probably right: her father had deserted the family when she was three, and her mother had married again—to a slightly younger man who had no interest in a stepdaughter—when Prunella was at the vulnerable age of thirteen. More than enough to engender a wariness about new relationships that might change life dramatically, or old relationships where trust might suddenly be broken. Unfortunately, knowing why she found it hard to form friendships did not make it any easier for her to do so.

Emma, a complete opposite in temperament, was her best friend, and had been for five years. And perhaps she *did* need a change and a challenge. They applied for the positions at the same time, and both were accepted. Prunella began to look forward to the adventure very much. A year in a place that she had barely even noticed on a map until now. An option to stay beyond the year if she liked it. Emma to share the hurdles and difficulties with. Two weeks until they were due to leave. . .

'I have someting to tell you, Prunella. . .' Emma's eyes were shining, her face sheepish but radiant. 'I won't be coming to St Anthony with you after all. You see, Douglas came round last night and we realised the whole thing was stupid. We're not going to put it off any more. The wedding's next week—almost an elopement. But you'll be bridesmaid, of course, before you go. . .'

It hadn't entered Emma's head that Prunella might have qualms about Newfoundland now that she was to go alone, and Prunella said nothing about it. She simply started having nightmares about wading through driving snow to get to work on her first morning at the Charles S Curtis Memorial Hospital, running hours late, making no progress, and dressed in an emerald-green taffeta bridesmaid's gown.

The wedding went off beautifully, the couple flew to Paris, and four days later Prunella took off for Canada, still pretending to all and sundry that she was almost as happy as her newly married friend.

There were two other nurses headed for St Anthony on the same series of flights, and Prunella followed the advice of the Curtis Hospital representative who had selected her for the job and helped with subsequent arrangements, and held up a placard at the airport with the names Leanne Southcott and Glenda James on it in order that they might all sit together and get to know one another. It was a very hard thing for her to do, particularly after she had fended off a persistent young man who had said his *first* name was James, and would he do instead?

She weathered this, however, and duly made contact with Leanne and Glenda. The girls, who were both from Glasgow and had trained together, made a few token remarks and then became absorbed in gossip about their own affairs. If Emma had been there, or if Prunella had been like Emma—able to bounce into someone else's conversation with a couple of outrageous questions that created instant focus—she might not have lost heart. . .But she wasn't Emma, and Emma wasn't there, and Prunella retreated into a shell that looked like prickliness from the outside but was really something much more soft and vulnerable.

Loneliness settled on her shoulders like a mantle and discouraged her new workmates, even though most of them were more sensitive than Leanne and Glenda, from making overtures and pushing beyond the barrier. She knew, having overheard someone use the phrase, that she was known as 'That quiet one', and the knowledge only drove her a little further away from the chance of reaching out. And the worst thing was that she couldn't help blaming Emma for what was happening. Two weeks wasn't a very long time when things were going well, but when they weren't. . .

'Too strong for you?' Rourke had to repeat the question before it made sense to Prunella. 'I asked if you were finding the tea too strong. They say we drink it like paint-stripper in these parts.'

'I'm getting used to it,' Prunella conceded with a smile. It was perhaps the one thing she *was* getting used to about St Anthony. That, and her work as a theatre nurse, which she had always loved and which was now the most absorbing and contented part of her days.

'Sorry about that,' he said. 'I wasn't thinking when I left the tea-bag in for so long. You should have said something.'

'I wasn't thinking either. And the cake's delicious,' she added quickly, in case her frank reaction to the tea seemed ungracious.

'Thanks,' he answered.

'You made it yourself?' It clearly *was* home-made, with a lemon and poppyseed flavour that was unusual and tangy.

'Don't sound so surprised,' he said. 'Men can bake cakes. It's legal.'

'It wasn't that you were a man,' she replied confusedly. 'It's more. . . I didn't think anyone baked any more, except people's mothers. Or people in chic wee London flats who do gourmet pasta sauces and brunch on Sundays, and that sort of thing.'

'And I don't fit that stereotype?'

'No.'

She was beginning to conclude that he didn't fit any stereotype. He was a Newfoundlander, he had said so himself, and had laid claim to a strong streak of regional temperament, but beyond that it was hard to place him. Surely he was well educated—he didn't fit her idea of a fisherman who had never strayed beyond these shores. Was he a teacher? An administrator? The hospital was the biggest employer of professional people in the town, but she had mentioned that she was a nurse there and he had not responded. In any case, she thought she knew most of the faces around the hospital by now and would certainly have remembered one as distinctive— and ruggedly attractive—as his.

Uncharacteristically—made bold, perhaps, by the unusual circumstances of the afternoon—she ventured to probe a little.

'The—er—fisheries have been going through a difficult time over the last few years. If you grew up here you're probably concerned.'

'Yes, it's hard to know what the future will bring. It starts to embrace wider issues, like the world-wide depletion of ocean resources.' A non-committal answer.

'Do you go out. . .do you fish much yourself?'

'Of course!' He grinned, then suddenly lifted the blue enamel mug to his lips and drained the last third of his tea in a couple of gulps, then got to his feet as if making an abrupt decision that it was time to get going.

Prunella scraped the legs of the camp chair nervously against the floor and crammed some cake into her mouth. The mug of tea was only half gone, since she had been sipping it quite slowly.

'No hurry,' Rourke said, seeing her haste. 'I've got to pack up my tools.'

'You're doing all the work yourself?'

'Most of it. It's a good way to spend my spare time.'

Then perhaps he *was* a professional fisherman. The season was short—plenty of time for a project such as house-building. As he packed up carpentry tools and swept away shavings from the kitchen, where he had been working, Prunella took her tea and wandered around. To her untrained eye it looked very well done, each join in the wood level and true, and the panelling that covered the stone walls smoothly finished.

The plastic that temporarily covered the windows was smeared and dusty, but it couldn't disguise the fact that every room would have a magnificent view of the sea. She finished her tea and packed up the mugs and Thermos, then stood by the sitting-room windows as she waited for Rourke, watching the waves pound and foam among the rocks. In a storm, sheltered here behind thickly glazed windows, it would be truly magnificent—as long as there was someone to share the sight with. . .

She didn't notice that he had come up to her until she felt a hand rest lightly and warmly on her forearm, and at once it brought a tingle of awareness to the back of her neck.

'We're ready to go,' Rourke said.

'Oh! Sorry, I was. . .'

'Daydreaming, I know.' He paused, then added gently, 'Although the daydreams didn't look like particularly happy ones. Is anything wrong?'

'Just homesick.' The confession, uncharacteristic in the way it voluntarily brought her closer to a stranger, came on a cracked note, and she picked unseeingly at the thick plastic that covered the window. 'I can't see, at the moment, how I'll stay here the year I'm contracted for.'

'You're contracted for a year?' For a moment his face donned a mask of something that could have been wariness.

'Yes, and I've only done two weeks,' Prunella answered.

'And yet home can't have been perfect, can it? Or you wouldn't have come away at all.'

The simple, teasing truth of this made her tears turn to a quick laugh. 'That's true. At times I was lonely in Inverness, too, even though I was born there. Perhaps I'm just a lonely person.'

'Lonely as well as homesick now?' His voice, losing its craggy edge, was still gently teasing. Then he stood back from her and studied her very seriously. 'No, I don't think you're a lonely person. I wouldn't say you were the all-night-party-type either, but. . .'

'Then what am I?'

'Like me, perhaps. You'd rather have one glass of very good wine than two dozen bottles of cheap alcoholic gut-rot. In other words, you choose your friends rarely and carefully, but you choose them well.'

'I'd like to believe you but, since you only met me this afternoon . . .'

'Shall I do a Sherlock Holmes and tell you why I think I know?'

'If you like.' Again she laughed. 'If it's so "elementary".'

'It *is* elementary. . .my dear Watson. It's your clothes. . .and I don't mean my pullover.'

'What about my clothes?'

'They're not new, and they're not flashy, but they're well looked after and the quality is top-notch. Angora mohair pullover, linen blouse, if I'm not mistaken, the kind of jeans that princesses wear, when they wear jeans. Am I right?'

'I do try. . . I'd rather have. . .a few good things than a lot of cheap rubbish,' she admitted, confused by his accurate gauging of her wardrobe. And he *had* noticed the blouse, which might be linen but was definitely on its way out!

'And isn't that what I just said about wine?' he pointed out.

'Yes. Only I'd never thought of it that way. It just seemed the sensible way to buy clothes.'

'And the sensible thing to do about loneliness here in St Anthony is to spend time with the people you meet in the daily course of things, and then choose the ones you want to have as your real friends.'

'What if they don't choose me?' she challenged, not fishing for reassurance or a compliment, but simply interested to hear what reply this unusual Newfoundlander would make.

'They'll choose you,' was all he said.

The dog was asleep when they returned to the Land Rover, but as they opened the doors he wakened and wagged his tail.

'He's going to be fine in a day or two,' Rourke said. 'But it was lucky we happened along.'

It was indeed, Prunella thought, and not just for the dog's sake. In a departure from her usual caution about new relationships, and *not* according to the plan she and Rourke had just mapped out for making friends, she had a definite desire to see this man again, and somehow it felt good to be uncautious. She was exhilarated, light-headed, full of energy.

As they drove she snuggled into the dark navy pullover that she still wore and thought to herself, Well, that's a guarantee that I'll see him again. I'll have to give this back.

He had relegated her own garment to a plastic shopping bag as if to say, you won't be wearing this again until it's been through the laundry. She dared to believe that he might have done this on purpose so that the pullover could provide him with an excuse for renewing contact.

'I'll drop you at the hospital, then I'll start asking people about who Rover might belong to,' he said. 'But I'll stop for petrol first, if you don't mind.'

'Of course not.' On the contrary, she was very happy to remain with him a bit longer.

A few minutes later he swung into a petrol station, and she stayed in the vehicle while he filled the tank; then he disappeared inside to pay and she turned to check on the injured animal as they had each been doing every few minutes.

This time she found that he was gazing at her with big eyes that seemed mutely apologetic. The reason for the apology was immediately evident. Very neatly in the middle of the old brown coat Rover had brought up his lunch.

'Oh, my goodness!' Prunella exclaimed under her breath. Something would have to be done. As a nurse, she wasn't overly squeamish about such things, but. . .

Before the mess could make its presence known to her sense of smell she opened all the doors of the vehicle and coaxed the dog out of the car, in case there was another bout of sickness on the way. He hobbled immediately after her as she gingerly picked up the coat and carried it to a water tap on the far side of the garage building, where another four-wheel-drive stood, having its tyres topped up with air. She smiled vaguely and a little self-consciously at the owner of the vehicle. He was slightly in her way. 'Got a problem there?' he asked as he stepped aside. Rover immediately began an ecstatic sniffing around the cuffs of the man's old jeans, and no longer looked ill at all.

'Sorry. . .' Prunella began.

'That's all right. I've got a catch of cod in the back

there. He can smell it on my legs too. He got a cut on that paw, did he?'

'Yes, and now he's. . .' She held up the coat and screwed her pretty features into a grimace of distaste, then ran the tap at full force to sluice the mess away.

'He'll be all right. He looks healthy.'

'Yes. . .' Then on impulse, since the man—in his forties and with a sandy growth of stubble—looked and sounded like a local, 'I. . .we. . .found him on the beach. You wouldn't have any idea whose dog he could be?'

'Dave?' he called over his shoulder towards the vehicle, and for the first time Prunella saw that there was a man in the back seat doing something with a piece of fishing tackle.

The brawny form climbed out of the vehicle and took his first look at Rover. 'Whose dog? Isn't that the animal that Conlan Donovan bought a month ago from some tourist? Yes, it is! Hey, Drifter! Drifter, boy!'

The response was instant. The dog attempted to jump up, yelping happily, then with pain as he came down too hard on his injured paw.

'There you are, dear,' the first man said. 'Drifter. Conlan Donovan's dog.'

'Thanks very much.'

Quickly she squeezed out the coat, which seemed perfectly clean now, and Drifter followed her obediently back to the car, to which Rourke had only just returned himself.

'I asked inside, but the girl at the till didn't know. She phoned a friend who——'

'It's all right,' Prunella said, proud of her detective work, although she couldn't honestly take much credit for it. 'Look! Drifter! Drifter!'

Again the dog panted excitedly and wagged his tail in no uncertain terms.

'Well done!' Rourke said. 'How on earth did you do it?'

Prunella explained the circumstances quickly, then finished, 'So he belongs to a man called Conlan Donovan.' She spoke the name triumphantly, like a conjuror pulling a rabbit from a hat. 'I thought you'd probably know. . .who. . .he. . .' She trailed off.

It was like a storm cloud crossing the sun. Rourke's face had darkened, his jaw was locked tight and a frown made a crease on his forehead that was as dark as his black brows. 'Yes. All right,' he said grimly, more to himself than to her. 'So he's Conlan's dog. That makes things easy. I'll manage it in the usual way.'

Prunella shivered and said nothing. The moment had opened a dark glimpse to her of some enmity in Rourke's life, and she didn't want to know what it was, didn't want to have it spoil the afternoon and their frank talk about loneliness and friendship. She saw that Rourke had reached to pat the animal again, as if to apologise for the fact that his master was Rourke's enemy.

When the man spoke again it was with a deliberate attempt to shake off the black moment. 'It's after five, Prunella—are you called Prue?'

'Sometimes,' she admitted.

'. . .So you probably want to get back to the hospital. Are you on tonight?'

'No, not till tomorrow.'

'What ward?'

'Not a ward. Theatre.'

There was a tiny pause, he took in a breath, then let it out again and said, 'Right.' It was a slightly off-putting response. Prunella didn't know what to say next, so she said nothing at all, and after a minute he spoke again. 'Do you specialise in that area, or did you just get put there?'

'Oh, no! I specialise. I love it. It's all I've done for the past two years.'

'What makes it so interesting?' he questioned casually, as if trying to fill in the last few minutes they spent together with some very neutral, easy conversation.

'Well, it's hard to explain to someone outside the world of medicine without it sounding as if I'm a wee bit ghoulish,' Prunella said. 'The human body is so interesting. It's fascinating to see the way we work inside, like watching the mechanism of a clock, only so much more complex. Every case is different, and it's quite miraculous what a surgeon can do these days. They're amazing people too. It sounds as if it would be gory, with the blood and all that, but when you're actually there at work it's not gory at all.' She stopped suddenly, aware that her answer to his question was growing too long.

'I'm glad you like what you do. That seems to be unfashionable these days.'

'Well, I don't always go on like that about it,' she said, blushing a little. He had turned to study her, a gaze of assessment, and it brought her into the hypnotic range of those sea-green eyes. He seemed to keep them permanently narrowed, as if accustomed to the glare of light on water, and it gave him the look of some predatory creature on the watch—a wolf, perhaps, or a lynx. 'About your pullover. . .' she went on quickly.

'Just leave it at the front desk in the foyer.'

'Of the hospital?' she squeaked, and knew it sounded too disappointed and very inane. This particular hospital had a very well-known and beautifully decorated rotunda as its foyer, and it wasn't likely that he could be referring to any other place.

'Yes, it seems easiest, doesn't it?'

'Yes, if it's convenient for you. . .'

'It's no trouble.' He gave her an odd look.

'I'll wash it, of course.'

'Don't be silly! It wasn't exactly clean when you put it on. Building a house is a messy job.'

'All right, then.'

A few minutes later they had arrived at the hospital— or, rather, at one of the staff buildings just beyond, in which Prunella had a small bed-sitting-room. She began to thank Rourke, wanting to say how much she had enjoyed the afternoon, how their talk by the unfinished window had taught her something, and how the day had had a quality of adventure for her after two lonely weeks, but she stumbled over the words, and before she had successfully completed the first sentence he stopped her with a dismissive wave. 'You've nothing to thank me for.'

'But——'

'I'll probably see you very soon.'

'Oh! Yes, that would be lovely. . .'

But he was already driving off as she spoke the last words and she wasn't even certain that he had heard. 'Probably see you'—ambiguous in its wording. Did he mean that he wanted to and would make sure it happened, or simply that in a place like this you ran into everyone sooner or later?

She watched as the four-wheel-drive roared away and realised that Rourke hadn't even given her a chance to say goodbye to Drifter, who was once again asleep on the now coatless back seat, an untidy golden bundle of fur and feet. The vehicle headed east and turned down a side-street with a speed and fluidity that suggested its driver knew exactly where he was going. Since there were less than four thousand people in St Anthony, this was hardly surprising, but somehow Prunella had got the impression that Rourke wouldn't be confronting Conlan Donovan directly in order to restore his lost animal to him. She wondered if she would ever know the story of the man's hostility. Was it town gossip, or a bitterly hidden secret?

The air was chilling down rapidly as the day began to fade. It was early June, so sunsets were late and drawn out, but as soon as the rays of light became slanted west they lost their warmth, and even Rourke's thick pullover was no longer enough. Prunella didn't want to go in, however. Out of doors there was the companionship of sky and sea, while her room always brought a return of loneliness.

From here she could see the small harbour, where white ruffles of foam had been teased from the blue waves by the fresh breeze. One or two fishing boats—small private ones, not the much larger and better-equipped company vessels—puttered across the water. The docks opposite the processing plant were quiet.

Around the harbour, the town stretched loosely. It wasn't a beautiful place. In this climate, much harsher than that of Scotland, although St Anthony was at London's latitude, too little vegetation grew to permit the softening effect of gardens, parks and woodlands. Bathed in the chill waters of the Labrador current, this northern tip of Newfoundland was almost tundra, and the conifers that grew here were scattered and straggling, their ranks thinned even further by the need for firewood.

It was the elements—wind and cloud, rock and water—that lent a rugged beauty to the man-made structures they dominated, and in winter snow and ice would mantle the whole landscape in a remote, glittering loveliness. Prunella wondered if she would last it out here until winter. For a moment she felt defeated again and ready to leave next week; then a stubborn streak in her rose to the surface to battle with the part of her that was a fearful prisoner inside loneliness.

'Even if I *don't* see Rourke again,' she said to herself,

'I'm going to remember this afternoon, and I'm going to find a way to be happier here.'

It was a strong resolution, and it brought her a quietly pleasant evening with another fairly new nurse named Eileen, originally from St John's, whom she invited to her room for a cup of tea. The start of one of the special friendships Rourke had talked about? Too soon to say. As Prunella fell asleep that night, however, it was Rourke the man, and not what he had taught her about loneliness, that filled her drifting thoughts.

CHAPTER TWO

'You seem cheerful this morning,' Helen Cobb said to Prunella as they prepared for surgery the next day. The senior theatre nurse, scrubbing for Theatre One, was also a native of Scotland and had married in St Anthony after coming here to nurse in her early twenties fifteen years before.

'Oh —' Prunella began, about to make a non-committal 'not really' in reply, then she overcame the desire to hide herself away behind such phrases and found a smile instead. 'Yes, I had a very enjoyable day off yesterday.'

'Oh, were you at the softball tournament? I couldn't get there myself.'

'No. . .' Prunella was ashamed at herself. There had been a series of social games at the playing field yesterday afternoon, with teams from two not-too-distant towns putting in an appearance. She had considered going, had listened to other staff making plans for the event. . .and hadn't done anything about it. 'I. . . I didn't get to the playing field. I walked along the coves and headlands and helped to rescue a dog.' Conscious that this sounded like a lame reason for a good day, she changed the subject quickly, saying, 'It seems like a long list this morning.'

'Yes, that's because Dr Donovan is back,' another nurse put in. 'General surgery and gynae oncology, and he's been away for three weeks, so there are two hernias that have been waiting for him.'

'Dr Donovan?' Prunella echoed. In North America they didn't follow the English system of addressing a surgeon as 'Mr'. But was the man Conlan Donovan?

Drifter's owner, and the man who had brought that black look to Rourke's face yesterday? There could easily be more than one Donovan in St Anthony, but it seemed a coincidence all the same.

For several minutes she worked mechanically as she prepared and checked equipment for Theatre Two, and was unconsciously going more slowly than usual, until Helen Cobb brought her back to reality.

'Here's Dr Donovan's index card. He's particular about a few things—he likes his gloves small and his blades long. It's all written down, and I'd get it right if I were you.'

The last words were spoken gently, but they were a warning all the same. The senior nurse must have noticed that Prunella's mind wasn't completely on her work. She looked down at the card, one of a system which detailed the likes and dislikes of every surgeon at the hospital, including visiting specialists who might only make an appearance for a few days each year.

There were several things that needed changing on the trays of sterile equipment she had set out, and she chided herself for forgetting to check the card earlier. Her mind definitely needed to focus itself on the task at hand. There was no reason to keep thinking about what had happened on her way through the foyer this morning.

She had parcelled the dark navy pullover neatly in a paper bag, and had simply labelled it 'For Rourke', since she hadn't managed to find out his other name. She had approached the main desk nervously, wishing Rourke had said something about when he would be collecting it and whether he would be known to the switchboard operator.

The rotunda that formed the foyer of the Charles S Curtis Memorial Hospital was decorated with a sweeping ceramic mural in eight major panels mainly of muted greys, blues and browns, depicting the landscape of

Newfoundland and the life of its people. Designed by Canadian sculptor Jordi Bonet in 1967, its quiet beauty and rich detail, in which Prunella was still discovering new elements, was something she delighted to look at each time she came through this way, but today for the first time she was blind to it, and wouldn't have noticed if one of the Inuit figures had suddenly winked at her.

'I have a parcel to leave here if I can,' she said hesitantly to the switchboard operator, catching her between two calls.

'Charles Curtis Memorial Hospital. . .No answer on extension 451? The doctor was there a couple of minutes ago. I'll try 456 for you. . . Is it labelled?' the woman asked, looking up quickly from her controls.

It was not yet seven in the morning, but there seemed to be a lot going on at the hospital already.

'Yes—at least, it's for. . .for Rourke. It has his name on it.'

'For Rourke, is it?' The woman's eyes narrowed in surprise. 'All right, just leave it here, then. I'll see that he gets it.'

'He didn't say when he'd be coming in. . .'

'That's no problem, dear.'

Prunella saw that the switchboard operator—Alison Harriman, her name-tag said—a dark-haired woman with an ample figure and hazel eyes, was weighing the parcel in her hands as if trying to work out what it could contain. She must be able to guess that it was a garment, but that evidently wasn't good enough. 'Any other message?' she probed, not hostile but definitely curious.

'No, that's all,' Prunella said thinly, wishing she dared to do some probing of her own.

As she had crossed the foyer she had felt sure that she was being watched, and on the pretext of straightening the skirt on her dark green dress she had glanced back towards the lit-up desk. A quick movement of Mrs

Harriman's dark head had told its own story and made Prunella wonder more than ever who Rourke could be, and where he fitted into the town.

The words on the index card resolved into clear print again. The heading, 'Dr Donovan—General Surgery, Gynaecological Oncology', was followed by neat notes in point form. Everything was clear until the last line, when whoever had written the notes had let slip a hint of exasperation. The words were in quotation marks and were followed by half a dozen exclamation points like a row of angry little soldiers:

'Don't ask, just *do* it!!!!!!'

Barbara McKay, circulating between the two theatres this morning, came up to Prunella. 'First patient's waiting. Can you do his IV? And Dr Donovan phoned to say he's on his way down from rounds. Dr Anderson is starting next door, and Dr Green wants you to get her scrubbed as soon as the IV's done. Are you ready with everything?'

'Yes,' Prunella nodded, speaking the word on a hurried in-breath. She *wasn't* quite ready, and it was a situation in which she hated to find herself. She usually started work fifteen minutes early to make sure it wouldn't happen, but, again, that stupid parcel for Rourke. . .

Feverishly she made a final check of equipment with Barbara's help, put up the patient's drip, and then hurried to help the resident, Karen Green, through the special washing procedure and into her sterile clothing. Dr Green cleaned the patient's lower abdomen ready for the hernia operation. The anaesthetist was ready to start administering anaesthesia through the IV line. Dr Donovan would be here at any moment.

Behind her, Prunella heard the swing doors open. She turned, towel in hand, ready to help the surgeon

scrub. . .and came face to face with the man who had
been on her mind all morning—Rourke. Dr Donovan.
Rourke Donovan. There could be no doubt of that. The
man wasn't dressed in a surgical scrub suit for fun. In
fact, he looked so incredibly right as a surgeon that
Prunella wondered why on earth she hadn't guessed
yesterday.

Then she remembered that Rourke had—deliberately,
there could be no doubt—fostered a very different
impression, saying nothing about his own profession
even when she had told him she was a theatre nurse.
Not to mention those falsely naïve questions about why
she enjoyed it!

In the moments it took to think all this her face had
been blank with shock. Now she schooled it into a
remoteness that made her fair Scottish skin almost like
marble, and her 'Good morning, Doctor. Everything's
ready for you,' was as blandly courteous as an
automaton's.

'Thank you, Nurse,' he said, and if she had been
hoping to embarrass him into some kind of apology or
acknowledgement in his tone she was disappointed.

Mechanically she went through the process of helping
him to scrub, and only when it was over and they had
backed through the swing doors into the theatre did she
register with surprise how smoothly they had worked
together. It wasn't always easy to do so. A scrub nurse
had to be ready with her hands or a towel at just the
right moment, had to slide gloves on to freshly washed
and dried fingers without fumbling. Sometimes a nurse
could develop a sort of blind spot about one particular
surgeon and would just never get it right. Every time
they scrubbed there would be a collision of elbows,
followed by an impatient phrase from the busy doctor
and a hurried apology from the mortified nurse. It was

the scrub's job to take the blame, too, no matter who was really at fault.

All the more reason to be on the alert, yet this morning she had gone through the motions with her mind far away and it had been one of the easiest scrub assists she had ever done. Not that that took the edge off her anger by any means. They were beside the patient now, and Rourke Donovan had greeted Dr Green and Dr Hughes in a cheerful yet businesslike way.

'Enjoy your break?' the anaesthetist said.

'Yes, the Toronto conference was good, and the house is coming along,' Rourke answered. 'May we start, Dr Hughes?'

The anaesthetist made a final check of his monitors and nodded. 'Yes, go ahead.'

Dr Donovan and Dr Green draped the patient, then the former turned to his resident. 'Dr Green, would you make the incision?'

The hour-long surgical procedure began. After spending the past two years exclusively in Theatre, Prunella had seen this operation many times. Although routine, it wasn't always easy. Once the different layers of tissue had been cut and held back with retractors it could be quite difficiult to identify the actual site of the hernia— the place where the wall of muscle had broken to allow the tissue to push through.

Prunella was familiar with the tiny, repeated hisses of the cautery equipment, which sealed each artery or vein with a tiny burn instead of the much clumsier and slower tying off that was done years ago. She had to be impressed with the way Rourke Donovan wielded the tool and then gave it to the resident and guided her in improving her technique with it. Dealing with those blood vessels was an important part of the job.

It was vital to check, too, that the area was left 'dry'— that there was nothing that could bleed internally once the layers of muscle and skin were stitched closed again. Instruments had to be counted and the count pronounced correct. If by any chance it wasn't it was routine procedure to assume that the missing item was inside the patient, although Prunella had never seen this happen. Finally Matthew Hughes, the anaesthetist, would begin to 'lighten' the patient, bringing him into wakefulness in a precisely controlled way by adjusting the medication that flowed through the IV.

It was a routine operation, but each one was different. Rourke Donovan was perhaps the fifth surgeon she had seen at work on a hernia, and she couldn't say whether he was the best. It wasn't that simple.

He certainly wasn't the rudest, though. 'Thank you, Nurse,' came in a steady tone at regular intervals, and only once was there a hint of annoyance—'No, that clamp's way too big'—reminding her that one of the notes on his card called attention to his preference in this area.

He did get angry with Dr Green, however. 'Shall I put in another retractor?' she said at one point, and his sharp rejoinder made Prunella jump.

'Don't ask, just do it.' The phrases at the end of the list on his card. She held her breath as he continued, 'If you need to ask then don't do it. If you're sure, do it and don't waste time. We're trying to establish some sort of flow here, Karen, and we'll never do that with your one-toe-in-the-water attitude.'

'I'm sorry.' The hand that reached for the retractor trembled slightly and Rourke sighed loudly. Prunella snaked a hand in quickly to hold a second retractor, praying it was the right thing to do.

'Listen, we're talking about operating styles,' Rourke went on, ignoring his scrub nurse. 'Another surgeon *will* want you to ask. *I* don't, that's all. Don't get so tense. I try for a relaxed atmosphere, and if I snapped at you

just then it's because we went through this before I went
away, didn't we?'

'Yes, and while you've been away I've been working
mainly with Dr Tregear——'

'From whom you have to ask permission to clear your
throat. Yes, I'd forgotten what my locum was like.
Whose style do you prefer?'

'Putting her on the spot,' Dr Hughes interjected.

'I want her honest opinion.'

'Does he really, Karen?' the anaesthetist put in again.
'It's risky to take people at their word when they say
that.'

'Your style works well,' Dr Green began diplomati-
cally, then more daringly, 'as long as the team is right.
You can't force that smooth flow you're talking about.'

'Can't I?' Rourke growled. 'My teams are *always* right,
in that case.' Then he gave a nod to indicate that
Prunella's help with the retractor was no longer
required. 'Thank you, Nurse.'

She pulled quickly away and was ready with the next
instrument before he asked for it. The fact pleased her.
Any way in which she could restore her dignity. . .He
had been *playing* with her yesterday. That was how it
felt. She had no idea why he had done so, but whatever
the reason, it put her at a humiliating disadvantage.

'Call up to the ward and ask them to medicate the
next patient, Nurse McKay,' Rourke said to the circulating nurse. There was a long morning still ahead. Plenty
of time for further chances to gain ground with the
man—or to lose it.

At noon Rourke was finished. Both hernias had gone
well, and a breast biopsy on a thirty-five-year-old Inuit
woman referred by the nursing station in Forteau across
the Strait of Belle Isle had revealed only a benign lump
of tissue that had been easily removed.

'That's always a good finish to a morning's work,'

Rourke said as he peeled off his gloves for the last time. He handed the gloves, mask and gown to Prunella, but had been addressing Dr Green.

She replied, 'I know what you mean, but I don't know why you used the word "finish". I'll be here for hours yet, and if a fully qualified surgeon gets to go home as soon as surgery's over then the quicker I get through my exams, the better.'

She pulled off a green cap to reveal lustrous red-gold hair, and then the two of them disappeared through the door on a shared note of laughter without acknowledging Prunella beyond directing a brief nod in her direction. She was alone, and her working day wasn't over yet either. Dr Cattecar was taking over this theatre for two scheduled Caesarean sections as soon as the cleaning team was finished, and that meant a whole new set of sterile instruments to get ready, scrub-suit packs to lay out, and surgeon's idiosyncrasies to prepare for.

She was still in a turmoil of mixed feelings over Rourke's identity. Was it reasonable to feel so angry? Was it foolish to hope that there was some decent excuse for his deception? Was it dangerous to be plotting his come-uppance if no excuse was forthcoming? With a heavy sigh of frustration she abandoned these questions as unanswerable.

'It's my own fault for seeing him as an instant friend,' she told herself. 'And for letting yourself find him attractive,' a deeper voice inside her said.

The something else struck her, and she couldn't understand why it hadn't clicked before. If Rourke was Dr Donovan then Conlan Donovan must be a relation. She saw again in her mind's eye that dark moment when Rourke had heard the name of Drifter's owner. 'I'll manage it in the usual way,' he had said. It had seemed a cryptic utterance at the time, and was even more so now that she knew a bit more about the man.

'This one's going to be a bit longer than we thought,' Matthew Hughes said to Prunella, signalling the moment when thoughts about personal affairs had to come to an end. 'Mrs Bailey has just decided that she'll try an epidural instead of a general.'

'All right,' Prunella nodded.

'Barbara McKay's calling Dr Cattecar to let him know. It means we'll have the husband in Theatre, too, during the actual surgery. He seems a bit uneasy about it, poor man.'

'They usually find it's not a quarter as bad as they think,' Prunella responded.

It was hard for anyone used to working in Theatre to remember quite what an alien environment it could be to the general public. The place was home away from home to Prunella—all the more so here in St Anthony.

The positioning of the placenta slightly over the opening of the cervix, a condition know as placenta praevia, had necessitated the Caesarean, and it was performed uneventfully. Both parents were nervous but well controlled before the surgery, and tearfully happy after it as they welcomed their eight and a half-pound girl, Louise Marie, into the world. Mrs Bailey was very happy with the epidural anaesthesia and chatted excitedly about her baby the whole time she was being sewn up.

'I'm so glad I didn't have the general,' she said as she was wheeled away. 'To be able to see my baby straight away. . .'

Immediately Prunella began preparation for the next operation, but relinquished her position as scrub nurse to a plump Nova Scotian girl, Liz Emory, at three o'clock.

Leaving the main hospital building, she passed again through the rotunda and found that Alison Harriman had come off duty on the switch and was about to go home. 'Rourke collected the parcel, by the way,' she said to Prunella. 'Just a few minutes ago, actually.'

'Did he? That's good,' Prunella stammered. She could hear the note of slightly curious mimicry in the older woman's tone now when she spoke the name 'Rourke'.

It must have seemed as if I wanted to announce to the whole hospital that I was on first-name terms with him! Prunella realised in horror. She managed a few polite words to Mrs Harriman, then they went their separate ways, the latter to the car park and the former across to the staff apartment building which had once, before extensive modernisation, been an orphanage.

Some medical staff lived here as well as many of the nurses, and it wan't a great surprise to Prunella to find Rourke heading towards her on his way out of the building. He raised a hand in greeting and she was about to respond, prepared to give him the benefit of the doubt for the moment. If he apologised. . . Then she heard the voice of Greg Mead, one of the hospital's two paediatricians, just behind her. . . .'How are you, Rourke?'—and she realised that Dr Donovan's wave hadn't been addressed to her at all.

The two doctors moved off, talking together, in the direction of the residence car park, and left Prunella fuming alone. Rourke Donovan's message was clear: Keep your distance. They were both back on deck at the hospital, so yesterday had to be treated as if it had never happened. She simply had to decide whether she would accept this. He was evidently one of those doctors who thought that the nursing staff were too low a species to associate with socially in an open way.

'In that case,' she said to herself through clenched teeth, 'why didn't he make it clear who he was yesterday?'

Still standing outside the building entrance, she saw the green Land Rover speed past on the road that led out to the cove where that magical little house was being built. It was a gorgeous day today, sunny and windless, so that warmth penetrated her dress and massaged the tired area between her shoulder-blades like a firm hand.

Rourke clearly planned to squeeze in a couple of hours' work at the house, and her breath caught in her throat for a moment as her mind's eye conjured a picture of the stone dwelling against its backdrop of boundless blue sea and sky. Yesterday she had dreamed that she might see the place when it was finished, but now she had no desire ever to lay eyes on it again. What could she do about her anger, however, short of hitching a ride out to that solitary cove and confronting him? Absolutely nothing!

Greg Mead came back from his car, carrying a bag of fishing equipment. Another doctor who fished. At the moment she was so angry with Rourke Donovan that this shared recreational taste was enough to bring a black look to her fine features. Unfortunately Dr Mead caught the full force of it.

'Whew!' he said. 'What have I done to deserve that?'

'Nothing. It's not you, Dr Mead,' she said quickly, pleased that he felt free to address her in such a casual tone. They had only met a few times in Theatre.

'Well, I won't ask who it is,' he said. 'But I wish you'd forget about it, because anger spoils those pretty green eyes of yours.'

'Forget about it?' Prunella echoed boldly. 'He's going to have to apologise first!'

'Ah, so it's a he, is it?'

'Really, it's nothing important, though,' she put in hastily, seeing that she could get into further hot water if he probed any deeper.

She was about to hurry inside, already regretting her bold response to this near-stranger, when he stopped her with further words. 'Doing anything tonight?'

'Going out?' she blurted, suddenly awkward again and fighting an urge to retreat into anonymity. 'No, I was just planning to. . .'

'A few of us are meeting at the hotel for drinks. Eightish. Why don't you come?'

'All right. Yes. That'd be lovely,' she heard herself say.

'You will?' He seemed surprised, and finished in a rather blank tone, 'Good! See you there.'

He went ahead of her and disappeared inside without going into more detail about the arrangements, which seemed a little odd. Prunella assumed she should walk there—it was well within the range of her capable legs— and hoped she would manage to set off at the right time so that she arrived neither first nor once the group— whoever it consisted of—was already too closely knitted together.

She spent the rest of the day in a state of mild agitation about the evening. Why had Dr Mead asked her? Was she looking more open and confident today? She only felt so in fits and starts. What should she wear? The purple dress? Or the black trousers and green silk blouse? Who else would be there? 'A few of us' he had said. Just hospital people? Rourke Donovan?

But this last possibility was too horrible to contemplate, so she convinced herself that it wouldn't happen, spent a contented couple of hours with a book, and chose the softly draped deep purple jersey-knit dress that brought out the green of her eyes and made her feel like a sea princess. Touches of gold jewellery, pink lipstick and dark mascara completed the outfit without making her look too dressed up for what was quite a casual town.

She set off at ten to eight, feeling that her arrival time would then fit the definition of 'eightish' and was pleased to find on entering the rather dimly lit lounge bar that

Greg Mead was already there, along with three or four other people. He detached himself from the group as soon as he saw her and came over to greet her.

'You came, then!'

'I said I would,' she answered evenly.

'Yes, but from what Rourke said——'

'*Rourke*?'

'Oh, I mean. . .' The paediatrician clearly realised he had said the wrong thing. 'Not that. . .'

'What does Rourke Donovan have to do with this?' Anger surged to the surface again and drowned shyness in an instant.

'Look, forgive me,' the young-faced doctor said. 'I've been told before that people can guess my shoe size by measuring the width of my mouth. Comes of working with children. They're so frank, and it rubs off.'

'You're going to explain, aren't you?' she cut in threateningly, her green eyes ablaze and glaring.

'Yes, yes. He suggested I ask you, that's all, after he said he couldn't come himself, and he told me to persist after the first no. When you didn't *say* a first no, I thought you'd just fail to turn up instead. He said you were finding it a little hard to make friends here.'

'And now the whole town knows about it. I'm not an object of——'

'Look, no one knows. We'll drop the subject right now.' He was part promising, part begging, and Prunella felt her anger and outspokenness ebbing. 'Let's go over to the others,' Greg Mead suggested, 'And they won't think anything odd, I promise.'

He took her elbow and she let him drag her across the room to where two men and two women were grouped at a table with amber-filled glasses.

'This is Prunella from the hospital, also from Scotland, for those of you who haven't encountered her,' Greg said, wiping his brow as if overheated by his recent scene with her.

'I *have* encountered her, but not on first-name terms,' said a man whom she knew in his role as Curtis Hospital's orthopaedist. Alan Kerson was his name.

His wife Sue, a maternally built redhead from Vancouver, seemed interested to meet a nurse from Inverness, 'Since my grandmother was born there,' and had soon steered Prunella into a conversation about handicrafts and Newfoundland folklore. Prunella recognised the other man, whose cheerful face was somewhat hidden behind thick-framed glasses, as dentist John Paddon, also fairly new to St Anthony. But she had no idea about the other woman, and the group had split into two separate conversations before she got beyond the information that, 'This is Kathleen'.

She looked interesting, with a fall of long dark hair down her back, deep blue eyes and a heavy freckling on her face that was surprisingly attractive against its backdrop of perfect creamy skin. She said little, however, and hovered back and forth between other people's talk, looking up to listen when something caught her attention, then staring down into her drink.

A succession of drinks, actually. Too many, Prunella decided after an hour. And they weren't light beers any more either, as the rest of the group was drinking. 'Rum and Coke,' was the steady command when first John, then Sue and Alan, went to order another round.

Nobody else seemed to be taking any notice, and Kathleen's behaviour remained respectable—no embarrassing displays such as those used to indicate drunkenness in films. But Prunella found her silence more disconcerting than a loud scene would have been. It wasn't a silence that came from shyness. Prunella was quite familiar with that sort.

No, this was too morose and too tightly controlled for

that. She wanted to go over to Kathleen, who was seated on the opposite side of the table, and reach out somehow. Twice Greg Mead threw a, 'Cheer up, Kathleen,' at the young woman—she looked to be about Prunella's own age—but Prunella saw that he hadn't really begun to gauge the fact that she was more than simply pensive or tired.

'For a start, there's too much stuff that's the *worst* kind of home-made. You know the sort of thing I mean—crocheted acrylic oven mitts. . .' Sue was still talking about handicrafts, and Prunella couldn't remain interested any longer. She made a token response and was just about to excuse herself and go over to Kathleen via an unnecessary trip to the Ladies' room when the girl shook the long dark hair back from its curtain-like fall on either side of her face and rose.

'Must be going—sorry,' she said with an obvious effort. 'Got to. . .' She waved a hand vaguely and didn't bother to finish—or couldn't get the words out.

'Steady on, Kath,' Greg Mead said heartily. He had the reputation of being a very skilled and sensitive paediatrician, particularly with newborns, but his understanding of adults seemed more limited.

'I'll walk home. Fresh air.'

'No, let Alan drive you,' Sue Kerson put in, with a display of protectiveness that Prunella saw at once was a mistake. 'Alan?'

He got to his feet, as did John Paddon. 'Yes, Kathleen, you must let——'

'Leave me alone, arright?' The Newfoundland accent was strong and the voice loud and uncontrolled suddenly.

Kathleen left the lounge bar at a fast, heavy stride. It was a walk made clumsy by her iron-willed effort to walk steadily, and Prunella suspected that normally she would move very gracefully.

'Should we go after her?' John voiced the group's uncertainty.

'We could follow her in the car without her noticing,' Sue Kerson said, 'just to make sure she's——'

'Without her noticing? On St Anthony's quiet roads? Don't be silly, darling,' Alan reproved mildly.

'Well, for a group of medical people you're a bit short on ideas about the situation,' the wife retorted.

'We're not going to do anything,' Prunella said, with an authority that took them all by surprise. 'She obviously wanted to be left alone.'

'Yes, but perhaps we should—er—override her wishes?' John Paddon frowned and blinked. He had put his glasses away and there was a red mark left on the bridge of his nose.

'Do any of you know her very well?' Prunella asked.

'No. . .'

'I'd met her once,' Sue Kerson said.

'I think she was disappointed that Rourke didn't come,' Greg Mead offered.

'Why didn't he?' Alan asked. 'I thought he was going to.'

'The doors and windows for his house were delivered today and he wanted to get started on a couple and get the rest safely stored out of the weather. There's a change forecast,' Greg explained.

'But if Kathleen needs help. . .'

'She's a local, isn't she?' Again it was Prunella taking the lead. Somehow she identified with Kathleen. Was the girl in love with Rourke? she wondered inconsequentially.

'Yes, of course she's local,' Alan answered, as if it were an irrelevant question.

'And none of us is,' Prunella said. 'If she wants help she must have other people to turn to—people who mean far more to her than we do.'

'Help?' Sue said. 'Now we're making much too big a thing of it. She was only a little drunk.'

'Yes, so let's leave her alone,' Prunella answered with a gentle finality that no one questioned.

In fact, she thought that there was far more to it than that, and that Kathleen's drinking was the symptom, not the cause of the problem, but there was no sense in arguing over the matter, and so the issue was dropped.

For ten minutes people made an attempt at returning to drinks and conversation, but there was an awkwardness now, and soon the little party began to break up. The other drinkers, most of them workers at the local fish-processing plant, were drifting away now too, and the red-carpeted lounge began to seem sparse and lifeless with its chairs scattered untidily about, instead of warm and friendly as it had at first. A full evening of cigarette smoke hung in the air, too, and Prunella's eyes were beginning to sting. When Greg Mead offered to drive her back to the staff residence she agreed gratefully straight away.

What time was it? Ten already. She was officially on call for emergency surgery at eleven, and, while it was unlikely that she would be needed, it was something to keep in the back of her mind, all the same. It was for this reason that she had followed her one low-alcohol beer with lemon squash or plain soda water for the rest of the evening.

'I'm glad you came,' the paediatrician said simply as they left the car and walked towards the building after their short drive.

'So am I.' Their feet crunched on the grey gravel.

'In spite of—er—the bad beginning. Rourke and so forth.'

'In spite of that,' she answered steadily, wishing he hadn't reminded her.

She would rather fall asleep pondering the enigma of

Kathleen than lie rigidly awake fuming about Rourke.
And she still had plenty to fume about! How dared he
take her on as an object of charity out of hospital hours,
when he wasn't even prepared to acknowledge her while
on duty? She had thought yesterday that he was genu-
inely understanding of her loneliness, and the confidence
he had given her had started to pay off already, but if
things went on as they had done today he would leave
her less sure of herself than ever.

As she lay in bed thoughts of Rourke and of Kathleen
muddled together and became washed over with sleep
until in the depths of a dream it became Kathleen who
was building a solitary house for herself, made of rum
and Coke bottles, only most of them were broken, and
when Prunella paid a visit with her dog—a most peculiar
dream-dog it was, too—the dog cut his paw quite badly
on the glass. . .

The telephone was ringing. Still three-quarters asleep,
Prunella jumped out of bed to answer it as if touched
from behind with a cattle prod.

'Quick as you can, Nurse,' said Beverly Patey, the
night switch, and Prunella managed a croaking response.

Feeling ill at the sudden awakening, she struggled into
her clothes and was on her way within two minutes. It
was five past one, and the forecast change had arrived.
It was raining now. The ambulance was unloading its
passenger as she arrived, and she was able to fling a
quick question at the driver as she hurried past. 'Is it a
road trauma?'

'No, suicide attempt. Woman cut her wrists.' She
remembered her strange dream, and the man's words
made her spine tingle with a horrible premonition.

CHAPTER THREE

'Get a move on, can't you?' Rourke Donovan's voice grated roughly

Prunella didn't reply. An apology would only delay things further, and in any case she was working as fast as she could. She simply clenched her jaw more tightly and went on with the process of assisting him to scrub. That smoothness she had noticed during their first preparation together—difficult to believe it was less than twenty-four hours ago—was gone now, and, although she was not yet fully alert after dragging herself out of sleep only minutes before, it was not her fault that things were clumsy. It was Rourke's.

He was much more tense than a surgeon would normally be in these circumstances, and Prunella was in no doubt about why The patient that was being prepped for surgery was dark-haired Kathleen, and she was obviously someone very special in Rourke's life.

It had been a chilling moment when Rourke had entered the operating theatre to announce his arrival and had seen the patient, already inert under general anaesthesia, as Dr Green had draped her and prepared her.

'My God, that's Katie!' His hoarse cry had cracked on its final note and his face had drained of blood until it appeared waxy and almost green under the bright mauve-white fluorescent lighting.

Kathleen Kuusinen had been barely conscious from loss of blood, and now owed her life to transfusion. Her left wrist was a mess, and Rourke had left an earlier road-trauma emergency in Theatre One to perform the

49

most delicate parts of the repair job that would restore tendons, arteries and veins to full working order. Her right hand was only lightly slashed in comparison, but still would require several stitches.

As they finished the scrub-in Rourke was beginning to master himself, but Prunella was nervous for him. A surgeon should not go into Theatre in this state. Risking another outburst from him, she began to talk—the only way she could think of to steady him. The fact that underneath she still felt anger and resentment about him had to be overlooked.

'How is it going next door?' she asked. 'I heard there were two people flown in from Port au Choix. A busy night.'

'A busy night?' he echoed, and she felt, as she tied his gown, that he was trembling. 'You're saying that as if we sold hamburgers for a living!'

'Yes,' she nodded steadily, moving to face him, making him meet her gaze and willing her green eyes to have some hypnotic effect. 'This is our job. We do this a lot. It's not a city hospital, so there isn't another surgeon to do this operation that's coming up. Whatever she means to you, you have to go in there as if it happened every day. So answer my question. How is it going next door?'

For a moment he shuddered dreadfully and then was suddenly calm. He took a long breath and said, 'The passenger had superficial lacerations. Dr Anderson handled them under local. The driver had a bit of liver damage which took some time to deal with. I did most of it, and now Anderson's tidying up. Dr Kerson will take over next, because there's a split femoral head and a mid-humerus fracture as well.'

'I hear it was a bad smash, so it's good that they've both come out of it so well.'

'Yes, it is,' he nodded, the words clipped but without anger.

Prunella dared to breathe again. He was fit to operate now and, although he hadn't said it directly, she knew he was grateful to her for the strong stand she had taken. Together they entered the theatre.

The operation took over five hours and was so finely detailed at times that it seemed better not to breathe in case the movement threw the surgeon's concentration off. Under anaesthesia, and white from loss of blood, Kathleen Kuusinen hardly seemed like the same woman who had stared so blackly into her drinks just hours ago. There had been a strength in her depression and silence then. Now, with the dramatic sweep of hair bunched under a cap and those dark blue eyes closed, she seemed weak and without personality.

The way Dr Donovan was working, the young woman might have been anyone at all. When he finally stood back, his part of the job complete, and said, 'We'll all take a break in a minute. The morning list will just have to run late,' there was no betrayal of personal involvement in the case, just the usual satisfaction of a difficult piece of surgery successfully completed.

The morning list did run late. The team scheduled for Theatre Two was the one that had just spent the night there, so breakfast was brought in and they ate it without saying much, each quietly attempting to regain some energy for the hours of routine surgery ahead. There were two vascular cases scheduled, as well as a perirectal abscess.

Taking long mouthfuls of hot coffee and munching on a buttered bread roll, Prunella could not help being very aware of Rourke. The night had taken its toll, since he had been called in to the road trauma at ten and hadn't got any sleep at all. He had had an energetic evening before that too, she remembered, working out at the house. He seemed paler today, and a spattering of freckles stood out on his nose and cheekbones in the same way that Kathleen Kuusinen's freckles had seemed to darken against the pallor of her face.

Kuusinen. An unusual name, and she couldn't place its ethnic origin. Was Rourke in love with her? It seemed more than possible.

If I had a man like that in love with me I wouldn't be trying to take my own life. Unbidden, the thought came to her, and she rejected it at once. Firstly, a man wasn't an automatic antidote to depression, which could have clinical causes connected to brain chemistry even when nothing in someone's life seemed to be going badly. Secondly, she still had reason enough to be angry with Rourke. He hadn't spoken to her since the surgery, hadn't thanked her for what she had done to calm him, but then he had scarcely addressed a word to anybody. Like Prunella herself, he seemed mainly absorbed in his coffee and was halfway through a second cup, pulling on it in long gulps and tilting the mug so that his chin jutted strongly and showed dark stubble extending to the column of his throat.

Would he blame her if he knew that she had argued against going after Kathleen last night? she wondered with a sudden pang. In fact, did she blame herself? The question had snatched at her thoughts whenever they were free, which during the operation had not been often. Now she had time to really think about the matter, and guilt and regret swamped her before she could fight them off.

The voice of logic told her that she *had* been right, that Kathleen would have fought and blocked off any attempt to help her. If the suicide attempt had been a cry for help—which seemed likely, since someone who was truly determined to take their own life usually succeeded—then Kathleen would have made that cry to someone she knew. A group of strangers would have been powerless to change her action. She would simply have postponed it until they had left her alone. Perhaps the one thing they could have done was to insist that she go to family or friends. In hindsight it seemed obvious, but last night it hadn't been obvious at all.

I'm not a psychiatrist, and I'd never met the woman before, Prunella told herself reasonably. It didn't make the sense of blame disappear.

'I'm going to Recovery,' Rourke said, cutting across her train of thought. The words were not addressed to anyone in particular, and a deep frown, like a jagged ravine across his high, intelligent forehead, spoke of his preoccupation.

'When will we start again?' Karen Green asked.

'Half an hour. I've told them to pre-med the first patient.'

Prunella drained her coffee quickly, realising that time had gone by and she should begin preparing equipment. Rourke left the room, shoulders hunched and green scrub suit creased and limp from the long night. He would wear a fresh one for today's surgery.

'I hear it was quite a night here,' Barbara McKay said to Prunella as they checked equipment together five minutes later. The circulating nurse hadn't been on call and had therefore not been involved in the night's work.

'Yes,' Prunella answered. 'Theatre One was ready on time this morning, though, wasn't it?'

'Yes, they've just started, so they may call me at any time if they need something.'

'We all needed the break in Theatre Two.'

'I'm sure you did. How's the patient?'

'It looks good, although she made quite a mess. There may be some permanent loss of sensation in the left hand. It was much worse than the right.'

'It must have been hard for Dr Donovan.'

'Yes, I think it was,' Prunella nodded. Evidently the surgeon's special relationship with Kathleen Kuusinen was a known thing, and it might further explain Alison Harriman's disapproval and curiosity over the matter of the parcel yesterday. Was it only yesterday?

They went on with the check, and had just completed it when Rourke's voice came behind them. 'Kathleen is asking for you, Prunella.'

'For *me*?'

'Yes.' It was clipped, and he made no response to the surprise in her tone. 'Don't be too long. We can't delay things much longer here. They just called down from Ward Five to see if they could send the patient.'

'Perhaps I shouldn't go, then. . .'

'Go.' It was an order.

She hurried along the short length of blandly painted corridor to the small annexe that was the recovery ward. Screened by a curtain from the other bed, which was empty at the moment, Kathleen lay with her arm still attached to a drip and her wrists bandaged and immobilised.

'I asked Rourke who the nurse was during my op,' she said weakly. Her voice was still slightly slurred and out of control following the anaesthesia, and her eyes drooped closed from time to time. 'I thought it might have been you, and I'm glad it was.'

'Thank you,' Prunella said evenly.

'You don't know. . .why I'm glad?'

'No, I don't think I do.'

'You were the only one. . .last night who didn't look as sh-shocked and prim as hell because I was drunk, and the only one who left me alone. The others made all the fu-fuss about driving me, but till then they hadn't even noticed. . .Well, why should they, I suppose? But you did. You noticed I was pretty down—I could tell.'

'Yes, I noticed,' Prunella nodded. 'But shouldn't you be angry with me for not doing anything about it?'

'I didn't want anyone. . .do. . .to do anything. Oh, I hadn't made up my mind then to try this stupid trick,' she added quickly, gesturing at her imprisoned forearms with her chin, which was a very strong one.

'So you're glad it didn't succeed?'

'I am now. Last night. . .No, I guess I never really meant to go the whole way.'

'You gave it a pretty close shave.'

'So it seems. It seems. . . I did.'

There was a small silence. Kathleen had made no mention of why she had tried 'this stupid trick', and why she had needed the oblivion and false solace of alcohol, and Prunella didn't want to risk frosting the tender shoot of friendship that Kathleen was putting forth by asking about it. For some reason she felt drawn to the woman— something in her face, her manner, and perhaps her loneliness, but. . .

'I have to go,' she said. 'There's a whole morning's surgery coming up.'

'I know. I promised. . . Rour. . . Rourke I wouldn't keep you long.'

'But perhaps when you're out of here we could. . .' Prunella stopped, not knowing what to suggest. To her relief, Kathleen stepped in.

'Yes, we should get together.'

'You see, I'm very new in town. I'm from Inverness.'

'I know—Rourke told me.' There was no self-consciousness when she mentioned his name. 'I'm living at—my mother's at the moment, and during the day I'm at my brother's looking after his two youngest kids while my sister-in-law works at the plant. You can phone me at either—Oh!' She looked down at her useless hands. 'I was going to write down the numbers, but I can't.'

'Doesn't matter,' Prunella said, edging away from the bed. She had been away far too long already. 'I'll visit you on the ward and get them then.'

'Great!' The keen blue eyes looked much happier now than they had last night, then they closed heavily. There had been a giddiness and an abruptness in her manner, though, and Prunella hoped she didn't regret anything she had said under the ebbing influence of the anaesthesia.

When Prunella returned to Theatre Two she found that Helen Cobb had helped Rourke to scrub during a break in Theatre One, and that the whole team was now waiting for her.

'Well?' Rourke demanded as soon as he saw her.

'I'm sorry, I'll be as quick as I can,' she replied breathlessly.

'Not that. Katie. How did she seem? No, don't rush. There's no one scheduled in here after the three on my list. It's routine and we're all tired, so let's take it carefully. You can talk and wash your hands at the same time, can't you?' The words said everything about how important Kathleen Kuusinen was to him.

'Well,' Prunella began, 'she's still fuzzy from the anaesthesia. Considering that, she was very lucid.'

'Was she talking openly about what she'd done?'

'Yes, she called it a stupid trick. I don't think. . .' She hesitated, not feeling qualified to make a sweeping pronouncement.

'Yes? What?'

'I'm not a psychiatrist, but I got the feeling that she won't try it again.'

The look of blazing relief in his eyes told her that this was what he wanted to hear, and when he spoke it was rambling and emotional, not his usual crisp style at all. 'I got the same impression, but I didn't dare believe it. I'm too close to her, and I felt so much to blame. When she stood me up on Sunday at the house I was angry. Those doors and windows could have waited yesterday. They were under plastic sheeting already, but I thought her unreliability lately needed a firm hand. If last night was the major crisis point. . . Still, there's a long way to go yet before she puts her life together.'

'Is there. . .something specific?' Prunella began, again with hesitation. She held a sterile gown ready to put on.

'Oh, very specific!' he answered at once. 'She's just been through an extremely messy divorce.'

With Rourke Donovan involved as one point of the triangle? Prunella wondered. He seemed to be finished with his interrogation and was suddenly impatient for her to be ready—which fortunately she now was.

As they entered the theatre, however, she wondered just how he had managed to trap her into forgetting her anger against him. He must think I'm a spineless little donkey, she said to herself, happy for him to ignore me when it suits him, and eager to tell him just what he wants to hear as soon as he asks for it. If he weren't my superior at work. . .

But that was exactly the problem. During working hours she had no choice but to take her cue from him. If she wanted an apology from him, or an acknowledgement that it was low of him to have stayed silent on Sunday about his connection with the hospital, she had to confront him on neutral ground. By the end of the day's surgery she knew that this was what she was going to do.

'You're going out to the stone house, aren't you?' Prunella demanded, her hand already closed firmly around the door-handle of the Land Rover.

It was the next afternoon, and she had postponed the promised visit to Kathleen Kuusinen in order to lie in wait for Rourke until he appeared in the car park.

'Yes, I am, but——' Rourke Donovan began, his blue-green eyes narrowed beneath a surprised frown and his tone cool and off-putting.

Prunella overrode his reluctance. 'I'm coming too.'

He opened his mouth angrily and took in a breath to speak, but she only gazed at him coolly, opening the passenger door as she did so, and after a few seconds he growled, 'All right, then. Make yourself at home, and fasten your seatbelt.'

After surgery yesterday afternoon she had climbed the single flight of steps to her room, too tired to care about Rourke Donovan or anything else. Today there had been another morning of routine surgery, including a partial thyroidectomy on a patient who had been flown on Monday from the town of Black Tickle on the Labrador coast, after being seen by the solitary nurse at the nursing station there.

Rourke was full of praise for Susan Bellamy's work at the station, but he didn't manage to find a friendly word for Prunella all morning. This hardened her resolve, and by watching the car park from her window—not troubling to conceal herself behind the rainbow-striped curtains—she had seen him heading towards his four-wheel-drive and had galloped down the stairs in time to place herself where she now was.

She wasn't quite sure what she intended to do next, and Rourke Donovan certainly wasn't going to help her. He looked very different now from how he had three hours ago when leaving the theatre area to make his afternoon rounds. Charcoal-grey tailored trousers and a white shirt and coat had given way to work-worn blue jeans and a Black Watch tartan shirt of thick flannel, both of which had enjoyed their share of cement smears, sawdust and tool grease. It was the way he had looked on Sunday, when she had felt so good about him, and when she thought back to that afternoon and his falsely casual questions about why she liked her work. . .

'You tricked me horribly on Sunday,' she said, the words coming all by themselves, 'and I want to know why. I want an apology too.'

'Yes, I thought you might.' He glanced at her, then looked back at the road, his fine surgeon's hands swinging the wheel to make a smooth curve. Why hadn't she seen on Sunday that they weren't the rough, stained hands of a workman? An image came back to her now of those hands encased in well-fitting leather gloves as he had tidied up his carpentry, and she remembered that there had been a whole bag of them—some made of thick, undressed leather for cementing work, others fine and soft for cleaner, more precise tasks. 'I thought you might,' he repeated lightly.

Prunella exploded. 'Well, you can damn well give me one, then, right now! You seem to think that just because you're an attending surgeon and I'm a mere nurse on contract I'll swallow it happily when you decide to disregard the most elementary courtesies. *I* happen to believe that outside of working hours—which we now are—we're as equal as——'

'Prunella Murdoch, if you'll stop that spitfire Scottish tirade for a moment,' he cut in, almost shouting, 'I'll give you your apology!'

'All right, but it had better be a good one!' she finished, feeling her sails slacken considerably for lack of wind. She had begun to enjoy the outburst so much that his apology might be almost a disappointment. She didn't usually enjoy such loud vocal anger, but somehow today she needed the release quite badly.

They were beyond the reaches of St Anthony now, on a rather rough gravelled road where traffic was a rarity. Low bushes and straggling conifers were the only vegetation except in isolated pockets where local people had found richer soil and came in summer to grow quick crops of potatoes. Rourke pushed hard on the brake and in a few seconds he had halted the vehicle, in the very middle of the road.

'It was very stupid and very thoughtless of me to say nothing about being a surgeon,' he said in a deep, steady voice. 'I intended to tell you, then as you went on talking about your work I found it interesting—and amusing— to hear what you would say to someone who was, as you thought, outside the profession. And I also wanted to give myself time to——' He stopped. 'Actually, that's all. It seemed interesting and amusing. I can see now that for you it wasn't. In fact I was regretful about it as soon as I came in on Monday morning. If I seemed to ignore you——'

'*Seemed* to!'

'All right, I *did* ignore you. I was uncomfortable.'

'Less so than *I* was!'

'Perhaps.'

'So in future——'

'In future there may again be times when I ignore you. Didn't anyone ever tell you that surgeons are like racehorses—too much temperament for their own good? I've got an important job to do. I can't always treat the whole team as if they're my best buddies. Another factor—although I realise this is no excuse—is that I was very worried about my sister on Sunday. I'm still worried about her, as you know.'

'Your sister. . .' she murmured.

'Have you seen her again yet?' he went on, taking no notice of her interjected query. 'She mentioned to me that you'd said you would visit her on the ward. Please do.'

'No, I. . . I haven't yet, I am intending to. I'll go tomorrow,' Prunella said, trying to speak normally.

Kathleen Kuusinen was his sister! Now it seemed

obvious, and she could clearly see the family resemblance—those freckles, the strong chin, the dark hair, the intense eyes. Kathleen's were blue, while Rourke's were sea-green, but they had the same fiercely luminous quality.

She felt so relieved and happy that she wanted to laugh out loud, and it was only later that she wondered uneasily if this relief was a clear danger signal that she was falling for Rourke much too heavily and much too soon.

'She needs a friend in this town who's not *from* this town,' Rourke was saying. 'She's always wanted to get away from St Anthony. She finds these dramatic escape routes, you see—so dramatic that of course they can't work out and she has to come running back. At fourteen she stowed away on a hospital plane. At seventeen she turned up on my doorstep in Toronto and was going to be an actress. For two months she sent out photographs to agents and auditioned for amateur companies and said bits of Shakespeare out loud in her room, then she fell for the oldest trick in the book—a sleazy snake of a man who needed some nude photos so he could launch her on an "international modelling career". Fortunately it went no further than photos. Finally at twenty-one she married a Finnish engineer who was in St Anthony for six months during some remodelling at the wharves. He wasn't a bad man or a bad husband by any means, but he was twenty years older than her, a widower with three grown-up children, and his job had him on the move every few months, and not always to the most interesting parts of the globe. His English wasn't wonderful—that was part of the attraction initially—but it meant that they couldn't really communicate. They say *nobody* can learn Finnish after the age of about ten——' He stopped abruptly. 'I'm rambling as if I'm on an analyst's couch.'

'No! Say it all. Say anything,' Prunella answered him. 'I want to hear it.'

'You liked Kathleen?'

'I don't know her well enough to say that yet, but yes, I was. . .drawn to her in some way.'

She didn't say that it was even more what she was learning about Rourke that interested her in this conversation. Until now she had thought him strong, intelligent, good with his hands. Now she saw that he could be vulnerable and confused as well.

'Well, to cut it all short,' he continued on a heavy breath, 'there were fights, Kathleen ran away from him and back to St Anthony twice—and running away from Juneau, Alaska, and Godthaab, Greenland isn't cheap. She had no money of her own, so she wired to my parents for it each time—my father's dead now—which left them struggling financially until those of us who could chipped in to help. Seppo was old-fashioned about marriage and divorce. He felt she had known the sorts of places his work took him when she married him and that a wife's role was to go with her husband, wherever that might be. It's not an attitude I share, incidentally. Things got very acrimonious. Kathleen had no idea what she wanted to do instead, or where she wanted to be. She's twenty-six now, the divorce came through two months ago, and for the moment she's here.'

'Have you thought of professional therapy? Here at the hospital, since there's——'

'Actually, no, I don't think that's the answer,' he replied very seriously. 'Although of course she'll have to have a psychiatric evaluation before she's discharged.' He was looking across at her, and one long arm was spread along the back of the seat so that his fingers almost brushed her shoulder, but there was no awareness of intimacy in those green eyes. She was a confidante, not a potential conquest. 'And I'm not saying that out of a squeamishness about mental illness,' he went on. 'I believe there's something in this world that's going to mean a lot to Katie—a profession, a vocation, a way of thinking, I don't know—but she hasn't found it yet. She's like a boat with a good hefty anchor, but the anchor's adrift, it hasn't snagged bottom and held fast there yet. She's not a boat with no anchor at all.'

'Perhaps the water's too deep for the anchor to reach,' Prunella murmured, latching on to his metaphor. 'If she can only steer herself into slightly shallower water. . .'

He laughed and flicked her cheek gently with a long forefinger. 'I like that,' he said. 'I'll remember it. Maybe I'll even tell Kathleen.'

A car came up behind them, making stones on the damp gravel road spit into the air. It almost shaved the side mirror off as it rattled past and reminded both Prunella and Rourke that the outside world still existed. He pressed his fingers to his eyes for a moment as if to shake off tiredness and painful concerns, then started the engine and drove on, before suddenly slowing again a minute later.

'Hang on! I must turn round and take you back to town. I'm planning several hours' work at the house and you'd be bored stiff.'

She wanted to say that she wouldn't be at all bored, would love to help or simply to sit and watch, but a warning signal sounded in her head: she would sound too eager for his company. Indeed, she *was* too eager for it. Loneliness was pulling her headlong into feelings for him that were reckless and dangerous and utterly unlike her. No, she must not suggest spending the evening with him at the house.

'I can easily walk back,' she offered instead. 'We've only come a couple of miles.'

'Nonsense. It's a very dull walk.'

'Then take me to the house and I'll walk along the coves and headlands as I did on Sunday.'

'It's after four o'clock. Too late for a hike like that over rough ground.'

'All right, then,' she conceded. 'That's nice of you, after I hijacked the car.'

'I'm glad you did.'

'So am I,' she answered in a low tone.

When they pulled up outside the staff residence there was no one about, and Prunella knew she wanted him to kiss her goodbye. She also knew he wouldn't do so, and she was right. He didn't even turn off the engine. In seconds she was out of the car, and he leaned across and slammed the door before she could turn round to shut it herself. He drove off with just a casual wave, and she had to school herself to do the same and then go straight inside instead of watching the vehicle until it disappeared.

I forgave him far too easily today, and I know why, she thought helplessly. It's because I'm falling in love with him. Oh, it's happening too easily. I'm scared of it. Something's going to go wrong. . .

CHAPTER FOUR

'It's good that you came today,' Kathleen Kuusinen said on Thursday afternoon. 'Because they're probably sending me home tomorrow.'

'Are they? That's good,' Prunella answered. 'They must be pleased with your progress.'

'Rourke didn't say much—typical big brother, just told me to stop asking technical questions—and Dr Mayhew told me far more than I ever wanted to know about haemoglobin. He's a psychiatrist. What business does he have to know about blood?'

'So Rourke's advice was right,' Prunella teased. 'Technical questions bring on boring answers.'

They both laughed, and Prunella marvelled at the change in Kathleen since Monday night. She was almost too giddy and cheerful, with pink cheeks and a sparkle in her eyes, as if her narrow shave had given her a temporary euphoria about being alive, which surely could not last. The Scottish nurse found herself thinking ahead, making detailed timetables for entertaining Kathleen, spending time with her, keeping her spirits buoyed up. The fact that Rourke had charged her to be Kathleen's friend made her feel responsible in a way that could bring guilt with it if anything went wrong with the young divorcee's emotional recovery.

'What are your plans, then, if you're being discharged tomorrow?'

'Well, Rourke says I can't go back to looking after Con's kids for a week or so, so I suppose I'll just putter about. If the weather's good I'll lie in the sun and get a tan—darken the background to these wretched freckles.'

'There's nothing wrong with freckles,' Prunella protested.

'Says you, who don't have one. Oh, they look all right on the Donovan boys, but we girls aren't fond of them one bit.' She lay back against the tilted-up bed and laughed again.

'It sounds as if you come from a big family,' Prunella said, hearing in her own voice an eagerness to know more about Rourke and the people in his life. 'Is Con. . .Connie your sister-in-law?'

'Con? No! It's another brother, Conlan. The eldest, and I'm the youngest. And yes, it's a big family—there are ten of us.'

'Ten? My goodness!' Prunella murmured but it was something else that had pulled her up short. Conlan Donovan. Rourke's brother.

She had almost forgotten Sunday's incident with Drifter and the mystery of Rourke's attitude to the dog's owner. She had realised on Monday that the two men must be related somehow, but, with everything else there was to do and think about, her conjectures on the subject had gone no further. Now, suddenly, it all returned to her—Rourke's thunderous face, the steel in his voice when he had spoken his brother's name—and she wanted very much to know what lay behind his dark feelings.

Kathleen was listing her brothers and sisters and quickly Prunella focused her attention again. 'So it goes Conlan, Marian, Alison, Deirdre, the twins—Devlin and Dermot—then Finlay, Rourke, Fiona and me. There's a span of twenty-two years between Conlan and me. The first three girls are married with two or three kids each, and so is Dermot, but Devlin isn't, and Conlan's got *nine*, for goodness' sake! So yes, you really can say we're a big family.'

'And do you all get on well togther?' Prunella asked,

shamefully aware of her own ulterior motives, which went well beyond the genuine desire to involve Kathleen Kuusinen in a good therapeutic talk.

'Of course we don't!' Kathleen answered easily. 'There are squabbles and sides-taking from time to time. It has to be that way when there are so many. And of course. . .' her face fell into more serious planes '. . .there's Conlan and Rourke.'

'Yes, I gathered. . .' Prunella hesitated. No, it really wasn't right to probe like this. She was no gossip-monger.

She looked around the room. Shafts of late-afternoon light slanted into the ward, which was on the southern side of the building and had not yet been modernised as some of the other parts of the hospital had. It was quiet in here at the moment, with one patient still in post-op recovery, and another not yet back from Physiotherapy, while the others were reading or sleeping. As a medical staff member, Prunella had been able to slip in outside of normal visiting hours. No one was listening to their conversation, but all the same. . .

'*That's* more than a squabble,' Kathleen was saying. 'In fact it's very bitter and very long-standing. I love Con—and of course I love Rourke—but he does have his darker side. I don't see how it's ever going to be resolved.'

She didn't try to explain exactly what the problem between the two men was, and Prunella made no further attempt at probing. Instead, she reached for the book on the bedside table. 'Would you like me to read to you for a while? I know you're perfectly capable of reading yourself, but sometimes when people are convalescing they like to be babied a little.'

'It sounds lovely,' Kathleen nodded, 'and if I close my eyes, I won't be asleep, I promise.'

'I'll keep that in mind. Where are you up to? What's

this?' Prunella opened the book. The dust jacket was missing and the gold lettering on the plain red cover was faded and indistinct.

'It's an anthology of children's stories, actually.' Kathleen gave a laugh that was slightly embarrassed. 'Now you *will* think I'm a baby! But I love good classic children's literature.'

'Don't be embarrassed,' Prunella told her. 'Isn't that the test of good writing for children? That it's just as interesting for adults? *Alice in Wonderland, The Water Babies, Just-So Stories*—they all pass that test, don't they? So tell me where you're up to and I'll enjoy it as much as you.'

'I've been jumping around. Pick something short, so you can read it all the way through.'

Prunella flipped through the pages for a moment, found an Oscar Wilde fairy-tale and began to read in a quiet, measured way. Soon Kathleen's eyes did close, but Prunella was enjoying the rather sad story for its own sake, so she didn't worry too much about keeping her audience awake.

Fifteen minutes later she spoke the final words and closed the book quietly. The woman in the next bed was looking and listening with a smile on her face. Kathleen lay back with her strong features as still as a mask. 'I'm not asleep,' she intoned through scarcely moving lips.

'That's the end,' Prunella said.

'Is it?' The eyes flew open. 'Then perhaps I did doze off.'

'*I* didn't, but I missed the beginning. You'll have to start again,' came Rourke's voice from behind Prunella's right shoulder, 'or I'll lie awake all night wondering about it.'

She turned around, startled into a bright smile that betrayed her pleasure at seeing him. Rourke, standing with his hand pressed against the door-frame, had to suppress a sharp hiss of breath at the picture his scrub nurse made at that moment.

Seated by Kathleen's bed, the first in the ward, she was framed by the window as if it were the backdrop to a painting—a plain backdrop of blue afternoon sky. Sunlight caught at her blonde hair, which was loose now that she was out of the operating area, and turned it to a spun gold so pale that it was almost silver. She wore a loosely draped silk blouse in autumn shades that threw a warm light on to her creamy skin and contrasted with the jade-green eyes that had so bewitched him on Sunday.

He still felt bad about that afternoon, partly because he couldn't fully explain to her the reasons behind the behaviour that had so angered her. Perhaps he didn't even quite understand it himself. When he had told Prunella yesterday about Katie's complicated relationship with the town of St Anthony—her attempted escapes, her crazy flights home—he had been uncomfortably aware that his youngest sister's feelings were not so different from his own.

Fourteen years ago when he had left Newfoundland for Montreal with a partial scholarship to McGill University and a dozen exalted career ambitions—medicine was not one of them—he had intended never to return to the isolated northern town of his birth. With the selfishness and independence of youth, he had wanted to shake off his family ties as completely as possible., Oh, he would send money, presents, letters, would repay his parents for the huge sacrifices they had made in order to get him this far. But live in St Anthony again? Never!

Then, after puttering around as an undergraduate and moving gradually in the direction of pre-med courses, he had found his vocation in surgery. Even then, as he had studied and begun to specialise, he had seen himself in

Montreal, Toronto, perhaps Vancouver, but not in Newfoundland.

Two years ago, however, had come his father's death. Fishing out of the port of Roddickton with a friend, when the ice in the harbour had only just broken up and snow still covered the land, Jim Donovan had suffered a stroke and had been brought to the hospital barely alive. Thanks to the first-class care that the Charles S Curtis was now able to provide, he had survived for three more months, long enough to regain good control on his right side and a large percentage of his former speech abilities.

When another more severe stroke had claimed his life those three months had done much to help Rourke's mother cope. 'We had the best talks we'd had for years, with him lying up in that hospital bed,' she had said more than once when Rourke was home for the funeral.

And so he had begun thinking about the story that all St Anthony children knew—that of the pioneer medical service begun early in the century by Wilfred Grenfell. When Jim Donovan had been Rourke's age a dog sled would have been his only mode of transport to the struggling Grenfell Mission Hospital in St Anthony, and care once he got there would have been primitive and ill-equipped, although resourceful and dedicated.

But there had been more to Rourke's slow and painful change of attitude than his interest in the hospital. He had rediscovered a need for the sea and the way it dominated every Newfoundlander's life, and a need for the rough sinews that were the bonds within his family— needs that he hadn't known even existed.

Eighteen months ago, very reluctantly, he had made the decision to return here as soon as a vacancy occurred in his field. With a rising reputation in Montreal and with the hospital's commitment to employing local people, he had known he would be offered a position if he applied, but had expected to have to wait several years before the opening offered itself. As it happened, though, he had only needed to wait six months. A year ago, therefore, he had suddenly found himself committed to the place, and he was still adjusting to the change and to everything his new life brought with it.

One rather niggling feature of this new life in very familiar surroundings was the open conspiracy among his three eldest sisters that he should marry as soon as possible. Alison, who worked four shifts a week on the hospital's front desk and switchboard, was the worst. It was one of the reasons why he was so keen to be able to move into the small stone house at Bellow's Cove. Out there, no Donovan could say that they were 'just passing and stopped in for a cup of tea'. If he wanted female companionship at the house, no one needed be the wiser.

He had made one decision that Marian, Alison and Deirdre would approve of, however, if they knew of it. He was going to marry a local girl. If, that was, this absurd determination to remain in St Anthony didn't let go of him one day as unexpectedly as it had taken hold. And, if he couldn't find the right local girl he would not marry at all.

That was why Prunella's appearance at the cove on Sunday and her innocent revelation that she was a surgical scrub nurse had thrown him off balance. He was a man who knew straight away when he was attracted to a woman, and he was attracted to Prunella Murdoch. Not that attraction automatically led to what he was looking for, but it was a tantalising beginning, which he would have enjoyed exploring and following through to its conclusion if he had still been that supposedly rootless young surgeon in Montreal. Now he didn't know what to do. . .

No, actually he *did* know! He should leave Nurse Murdoch strictly alone! She didn't fit the criteria, cool green eyes and warm, careful personality notwithstanding.

The trouble with you, Rourke Donovan, he said to himself sardonically, is that you're a contrary animal. You've decided you can't have the woman, and that only makes you want her more.

A light flush had crept to her cheeks now. She knew he was studying her, must know that he wanted her. And he didn't think she was indifferent to him either. He cursed himself for handling this so badly these past few days. No wonder the girl had been angry and confused! She wasn't the kind of person who deserved bad treatment, if he was any judge of character.

Still, the sooner he could get her out of his system, the better. He had two strategies that should work. And I'd better get started on both of them as soon as possible, was his conclusion.

'Don't you have work to do?' Kathleen was saying to him.

'You're the last patient on my round,' he told her.

'And it's not even four o'clock! I didn't know doctors got to go home so early.

'I started at six,' he answered drily, 'and I haven't had lunch. *And* I'm on call tonight.'

'No need to be so defensive! I'll concede that you probably earn your salary.'

'That's generous of you.'

Prunella stayed silent during this brother-and-sister banter. She was still flushed and disturbed in the aftermath of that long look Rourke had given her, his blue-green eyes alive behind the screen of his thick dark lashes. It had created a disturbing awareness in her, and a strong desire to drown in his gaze as close to him as she could get. She had stayed in the low chair, of course, resisting the need to go to him. What had his own need been, though? she wondered.

After several minutes she turned her attention to what Kathleen and Rourke were saying, and they stopped talking about family gossip and started discussing films instead. There was a video shop in St Anthony now, and their sister Deirdre liked to turn an evening in front of the VCR into a small party, it seemed, with drinks beforehand and supper afterwards.

'She's having one on Sunday night, Prue,' Kathleen said. 'You'll have to come.'

'Won't I make it too much of a squeeze in a small living-room?' she answered uncertainly, feeling her usual wariness about people.

'Nonsense!' Kathleen exclaimed spiritedly. 'Always room for one more—that's Deirdre's philosophy.'

'Hmm. . .But isn't she having Alison's mob this week?' Rourke said. 'And Mum, and Finlay and his girl of the moment, as well as Meg and myself. I make that——' he counted quickly '—fifteen, including you, Katie. It might not be Prunella's idea of a fun evening, squashed into a room with five teenagers, six adult Donovans and four assorted associates.' He made it sound very facetious, but Prunella felt sure that he didn't want her to come. Had she been wrong about the awareness in Rourke's gaze, then? And who was Meg? Not another one of the Donovan sisters, if she had remembered their names correctly.

'It *is* fun, Prunella, I promise,' Kathleen said, seeming unaware of the undercurrent in Rourke's words. Perhaps it was Prunella's imagination, her usual mistrust of any friendship that seemed promising.

'I'll. . . I'll check my schedule.' It was a stupid thing to say. She knew she wasn't working that night. She wasn't even on call.

'And, if you're free, you'll come? Great!'

'For now, though,' Prunella went on 'I'd better get

going. I have laundry in a dire state and a letter from
my mother to answer.'

She rose and smoothed the front of her black spring-
weight wool skirt with palms that threatened to dampen.
For the moment she had had enough of the disturbing
effect of Rourke's company.

Unfortunately, she could not make her escape so
easily.

'I'd better be going myself, Katie,' he said. 'Official
visiting hour is almost upon us, and I don't want to get
buttonholed by gangs of my other patients' relatives.'

'Oh, Rourke!' sighed his sister.

'I'm sure there'll be a big Donovan contingent to fill
the yawning void of my absence.'

'Don't tease! You know you're my favourite brother.'

'All right, and the feeling's mutual, kid sis, but a
man's got to do what a man's got to do—meaning some
carpentry out at the house, if I'm to be living there by
the end of summer.'

'OK, do some work on my spare room, then.'

'*Your* spare room? That sounds ominous,' he growled.

Katie stuck out her tongue and Prunella laughed.
Outside in the corridor, she found that Rourke was
walking beside her, although he had stayed in the ward
a moment longer than she had done, in order to bestow
a brotherly kiss on Kathleen's forehead and a supportive
squeeze on her shoulder.

'What did you think?' he asked her as soon as they
were well out of earshot of the ward.

'She seems very chirpy,' Prunella answered.

'Too chirpy.' Rourke added her own unspoken quali-
fication. 'And very kid sister. She must be about your
age. . .'

'I'm twenty-four.'

'Really? You look twenty-four, yes, but you seem a
little more mature. That only makes it clearer that

Katie's taking refuge in her behaviour. She can seem, and be, very mature at times.'

'Are you worried, then?'

'Not necessarily. Just alert, and. . .can I ask. . .?'

'Of course I'll be alert too.'

They entered the foyer and Prunella darted a quick glance over to the lit-up main desk. Mrs Harriman wasn't on today. Good! She was self-conscious enough as it was about the fact that she was with Rourke. They had already passed Alan Kerson, who had given them a look of interest and curiosity—or so she had interpreted it.

Once outside into the bright day, she prepared to separate from him as soon as possible with an excuse about needing to get to the post office for stamps, but he held her back with a question that could not go unanswered. 'Shall we do something together on Saturday?'

'Oh. Yes, that would be nice,' she blurted gruffly, swept with a confused tide of pleasure and apprehension. 'What were you thinking of?'

'Have you seen our local Vikings yet?'

'You mean the historic site at L'Anse-aux-Meadows? No, I haven't had transport. I've been wondering how I'd get there.'

'You'd like to go, then? I'm on call, but it will be within beeper range. What about you?'

'I'm not on call at all.'

'Then we can afford to go that far. Shall we say ten?'

'That'd be fine.'

'I'll bring a picnic and we'll make a day of it, stop at a couple of other places.'

'What can I bring to contribute?'

'Just yourself.'

'But——'

'Seriously,' he said, and as she opened her mouth to

protest again he reached out and touched a long forefinger against her lips. His warmth against her mouth
sent a tingle through her as much as if it had been a kiss,
but the finger was gone again in an instant. It had done
its work in silencing her, however, and when he turned
from her and broke into a rapid stride, thrusting his
hands into the pockets of the light jacket he wore, she
could barely find a response to his, 'See you later, then.'
Saturday seemed too far away.

'I think it's going to clear,' Rourke said as they walked
to the Land Rover. 'Look over to the west. The fog is
thinning and the cloud's breaking up. If this breeze
swells a little the whole lot will get blown out to sea and
we'll have a glorious day.'

'By afternoon, do you think?' Prunella said.

'In an hour, girl! Weather's changeable in these parts.'

He was right. By the time they had reached the tiny
village of St Lunaire the fog was only a weird grey
presence far out to sea, and overhead the sky was almost
perfectly clear. After the week's work in surgery, with its
strong, hot artificial light and meticulously detailed
focus, it felt good to both of them to be out in the fresh
air.

'Mind if I have the window down?' Rourke said.

'Not at all. I'd love to blow the cobwebs away a little,'
Prunella answered, winding hers down several inches as
well.

'Not worried about your hair?'

With a laugh she reached behind her head and lifted
it in a silky handful off the back of her neck. 'Oh, it'll be
a tangled mess by the end of the trip, I'm sure, but I can
disappear with a comb into the Ladies' room at the park
visitors' centre and sort it out again, can't I?'

'Or you can leave it in a tangled mess. It's quite an
image. That fine blonde stuff——'

'*Stuff?*'

'Locks, tresses. . . Those fine blonde *tresses*, if you insist, *mademoiselle*, must look like cotton candy when they're mussed around a little.'

'Maybe,' she conceded.

He didn't make any further comment, simply shifted in the driver's seat and stared ahead at the road. It was winding and slow at this point, with glimpses offered constantly of islands, coves and jutting cliffs as well as tiny scattered settlements. Prunella would have liked to ask the names of the islands, but when she glanced across at him she saw that he was frowning and lost in thought, so she said nothing, wondering what in their recent frothy exchange could have triggered off this clear change in mood.

When he spoke again at last, though, it was worth the wait. 'Look,' he said. 'Out just beyond the bay. Is that your first iceberg?'

'Where? Oh, yes! And isn't that another one a bit farther out?'

'Looks like it.'

'Oh, it's magnificent!'

'Yes, it's a big one, and nice and close. We can probably get even closer if you like.'

'Yes, please!'

'I think if we turn off towards Straitsview. . .'

He took an unpaved road and wound his way to its end, then picked a way for them both on foot to a headland where the brisk wind made Prunella hug her crimson windproof jacket closely around her. The iceberg seemed very close now.

'I think it's going to beach itself on Quirpon Island,' Rourke said.

'It's beautiful.'

The ice glistened blue-white in the bright light, and rose in a sheer cliff at least thirty feet high on one side, but sloped sharply almost to the water level on the other, so that it had the triangular shape of a sail. As they watched, a large chunk on one side slid into the water amid a hiss of ice particles and was lost to sight.

'Yes, it is beautiful,' Rourke said. 'But, like most things around here, it's dangerous as well.'

'Yes, that's well known,' Prunella answered. 'Ships passing through the Strait of Belle Isle in a fog and looming up against one of these. . . I'm sure there are a hundred heroic stories of wrecks and rescues. . .But do we have to think of the danger today?'

'No, we don't. I'll tell you an ambition of mine instead—to see these from the air as they float down the Labrador coast. I'm sometimes envious of the personnel who are involved in Medevac flights.'

'But haven't you yourself ever had to fly in a Medevac emergency?'

'It will happen some day, I suppose, but it's rare for someone in my position. And I've only been here a year.'

'A year? Somehow I thought it was longer,' she said.

'You'd have a greater chance of flying yourself.'

'Yes, we were told when we got the job that we could do a two-day course in emergency work after we've been here for three months and then be rostered on call for nurse escort duty in addition to our normal hours.'

'Do you think you will?'

'I haven't decided yet. Leanne and Glenda seemed very keen on that side of it, but I thought I'd wait and see.'

'Glenda? Is that Glenda James?'

'Yes. We flew over from Scotland together, but I haven't seen much of her since.'

He didn't pursue the subject and she wondered why the casual mention of the girl from Glasgow had interested him. Nothing important, probably.

'If I *do* fly I'll stow you away on board some time

when the weather's right,' she promised lightly. 'And we'll see the icebergs in the Labrador current together.'

'It's a deal.'

They returned to the car and drove the remaining distance to the World Heritage site at L'Anse-aux-Meadows. The reconstructed Viking huts, made of piled-up sods of earth and grass, stood in the midst of green, meadow-like terrain that none the less had a bleakness and loneliness about it.

'Why here, I wonder?' Rourke murmured. 'I know the climate was milder in the tenth century, but. . .'

'Yes, it must have been frighteniong to be so far from home,' Prunella said.

'And if it hadn't been for a Norwegian archaeologist, who was convinced that somewhere there had to be proof that the Vikings reached North America. . .'

'Why? Was it only discovered quite recently?'

'Yes, in the early sixties. Till then it had only been theory that the Vinland legends were based in solid reality. My mother met Helge Ingstad and, like a lot of people, thought he was crazy with his questions about whether she'd seen any bumps and ridges in the grass around this region. When old George Decker, who'd lived within a stone's throw of this place all his life, said that yes, of course there were some odd-shaped mounds here and what was all the fuss about? it took a while for the locals to take the digging project seriously.'

'It's very well presented now, though.'

'Yes, after a lot of work and international interest. Let's take in the visitors' centre first, shall we?'

The spacious wooden building contained exhibits relating to Norse culture in Scandinavia, Iceland, and Greenland, as well as information about the local site. There was a film about the discoveries at L'Anse-aux-Meadows, and from the visitors' centre a boardwalk led to reconstructed sod huts as well as the grassy shapes of ruined dwellings returned to much the same state as George Decker had known them.

Rourke and Prunella did not speak much as they wandered around the site. It was still too early in the tourist season for there to be many visitors, so they had the place almost to themselves, and silence was better, somehow, in this serene, history-laden spot.

'Can you imagine yourself as a Viking woman, working away with that spindle whorl they found during the dig?' Rourke said softly as they stood inside the cool, damp rectangle that was a reconstructed hut.

'It must have been dark for that sort of work,' Prunella answered, equally softly. 'Perhaps she sat in the sun whenever she could.'

'I'm sure she did.'

'Looking out at the water and wondering when she'd go back home to Greenland, or whether she'd stay here and have children and see a whole colony grow here.'

'You're too romantic,' he teased gently, flicking her on the cheek with his finger. 'Think of the smoke and smell inside this place when they were shut in for winter.'

'Yes, but think of the human warmth as well. . .'

'What? Huddled together under bearskin rugs and thick woollen cloaks?'

'It could have a certain charm. Don't destroy my illusions by telling me that the bearskin would still smell of bear!'

'All right, and if you ever wanted to experience bedding down among a tangle of fur blankets perhaps I'd be romantic enough to want to share in the experiment.'

She laughed, but was uneasy about the way he was teasing her. He stood there, leaning against one of the thick columns of raw wood that supported the framework of the roof, and he was watching her. Could he guess that the elemental image of sharing such a primitive bed with him had brought a strong surge of awareness and desire to every nerve in her body? She hoped not.

'Mm, I need the open air,' she forced herself to say quickly. 'I hope none of these Vikings suffered from claustrophobia. If I ever live in a sod hut it's going to have to have windows and more than one door!'

The laboured complaint got her safely back into the sunshine, and she walked on rapidly without waiting for Rourke. She needed to be a safe distance from him for a while—several metres at least. Perhaps he felt the same. At any rate, he made no attempt to catch up to her, and when she looked back she found that he had stopped to take a close look at the construction of the wooden fence that surrounded the reconstructed dwellings. She went on a little further, but he was still at the fence, so she sat down with her feet dangling over the edge of the raised boardwalk and waited for him.

'Sorry about that,' he said when he caught up to her again. 'I was thinking about my place and whether I should fence it.'

'A fence doesn't seem to fit your place somehow,' Prunella said.

'Yes, that's what I decided.' He reached a hand down to her and helped her up, then said, 'Time for lunch?'

'Very much so.'

'You haven't asked about what I've brought.'

'No, there's been too much else to talk about, hasn't there?' she answered easily.

For some reason it was the wrong thing to say. His brow darkened and impatiently he flicked away a strand of hair that had fallen forward across his slightly freckled nose. What he muttered under his breath she didn't catch and didn't ask him to repeat. A moment later he said roughly, 'Well, it's fish.'

'Pardon?' Aware of his sudden black mood, she wasn't

thinking about the picnic any more, and his statement
didn't make sense at first.

'I said I've brought fish. Salmon. Must be just about
the first catch of the season. And the accompaniments,
obviously. Caught it this morning. We'll grill it over my
hibachi barbecue. Hope that suits you.' His tone seemed
to imply that he actually hoped it *didn't*

'It sounds terrific,' she answered lamely.

Without speaking, they drove away from the heritage
site and found a sunny yet sheltered spot among some
small fir trees in the nearby provincial park, and Rourke
set up the tiny barbecue with its fuel of charcoal and its
metal grill on top. He had already wrapped the fish in
foil and had brought it in a cooler, resting on a bed of
ice. There was crusty wholemeal bread as well, lemon
butter and a tossed green salad. Fresh fruit and a bottle
of dry white wine, also chilled on the ice, completed the
meal. Although each part of it was very simple, the
thought of those pure fresh tastes had Prunella's mouth
watering.

'How can I help?' she asked as Rourke poured a little
starter fluid on the coals to get them going.

'By sitting and enjoying the sun. Summer's almost
over.'

'But it's hardly begun!'

'Well, that's Newfoundland for you. I hope you didn't
come here to get a tan.'

'Hardly,' she laughed. 'I'm looking forward to trying
some winter sports in a few months.'

'So you think you will last the year out after all?' He
looked up from where he stood over the barbecue,
matchbox in hand ready to put a light to the coals.

'Yes, I. . .things have got better over the past week,'
she said confusedly, afraid that he would guess how
much of the change in her feelings was due to him.

'Good. I'm glad. Perhaps you'll even extend for a second year.'

'Oh, I doubt that,' she said very firmly, frightened at the idea of looking that far ahead. For the moment she just wanted to enjoy today, untroubled by questions of the future.

Rourke must have found it a dampening response. He didn't say anything further, and punctuated her comment only by the crack and hiss of the match lighting. Flames sprang up over the charcoal, and while he waited for them to die down he opened the wine, sliced lemon and tossed a vinaigrette dressing through the salad.

His touch with the food was as deft and sure as his touch on a patient in surgery, and unbidden the thought came to her, I wonder if he does everything this well. His touch on a woman's flesh, for example. . . It was a dangerous train of thought, but as he moved near her, dressed in dark grey gabardine trousers and a light cashmere sweater above a pale shirt, she found that she couldn't dismiss or repress her physical awareness of him. He was still frowning and silent, clearly absorbed in thoughts that weren't entirely positive, but unfortunately his craggy face didn't lose any of its charm when chiselled into sombre planes.

After several minutes the coals were ready and he laid the silver-wrapped fish on the grill carefully. 'Now, if I've managed to wrap this well enough, the thing will poach in its own juices without leaking,' he said.

'It's going to be fantastic,' Prunella said.

To her relief, he looked across at her and smiled. He seemed to be a man of changeable moods, and it was disconcerting. 'Then it was worth the effort of catching it,' he said.

'Yes; you must have gone out early.'

'Five, and afterwards I made rounds. But I'm used to it.'

The meal was everything it promised to be. With the day's warmth at its height, it was delightful to stretch out on a picnic rug laid on top of a bed of soft grass and aromatic fir needles, and linger over the food. The glass of wine she sipped had a deliciously drowsifying effect too, and neither of them seemed in a hurry to have the picnic come to an end.

When Rourke rolled lazily towards her it felt so right that she didn't even hesitate. Those arms around her, moulding every curve of her slim figure, his hands stirring every pulse in her to life. . . It was exactly what she wanted, and after the weeks of loneliness she had just passed through his touch released her in a gush of joy and passion.

His kiss was expert, teasing at first as his fingers teased at her hair, then deeper and more demanding. Her response was equal to his, and her hands delighted in the firm feel of his muscles and the texture of his skin, slightly roughened already since his morning shave. She threaded curious fingers through his thick dark hair and found it clean and silky and scented with a musky shampoo, and when she traced her tongue and nuzzled her nose and lips into the curve of his neck she was enveloped in a salty maleness that quickened her pulses even further.

Their exploration of each other went on for a long time, until she was swollen with warmth and desire, and sensed that he was the same. There seemed no reason for it to come to an end, no one there to interrupt them, no calls on their time back in St Anthony. Longing and apprehension began to battle within her. Her body told her clearly how far it wanted to go, but her emotions were not yet ready to follow, and she struggled to find a way to let him go, even while her skin still wanted to press against him.

Then suddenly she felt a chill, and it took several

moments for her to realise that a cloud had crossed the
sun, blotting out the day's warmth with incredible
swiftness. It seemed to chill away the warmth of their
passion at the same time, and she wasn't surprised when
he pulled away from her seconds later, breathing heavily,
and pulled himself into a sitting position with his broad
back towards her like a forbidding wall.

Neither of them spoke. The transition of mood was far
too sudden, and she knew that he was struggling as hard
as she was to restore the world to its proper equilibrium.
While they sat there, still in silence, the sun came out
again, but its warmth did not feel the same. Prunella's
head had begun to feel heavy after the wine, which she
didn't normally drink during the day.

'Is there any water?' she asked, her voice coming out
rustily. It was awful to have to speak, but something had
to break the silence.

'Yes, in the Land Rover. I'll get it.' He was on his feet
immediately, as if relieved that she had found this
mundane way to break the tension. He strode across to
the vehicle, parked some twenty metres away, and
returned with a plastic water bottle and two aluminium
cups. 'Looks as if this good weather was only a flash in
the pan,' he said, still speaking in a brisk, impersonal
way.

'So it does.' Prunella looked at the sky to the west and
saw purple clouds piling themselves there. 'The sky
looks ominous.'

'We should pack up, then. Don't want to get caught
in a storm.'

'No,' she agreed, thinking inwardly, What's happened
to us? We're talking like polite strangers. It's as if we
haven't got closer to each other today at all.

And half an hour later, when he dropped her at the
hospital residence, this impression had not changed.
'You're not coming in?' she said. The engine was still

idling. 'To your flat, I mean,' she added hastily, suddenly realising that it sounded as if she meant her own place.

'No, there's work I want to get done at the house. I've got plumbing and electrical people due to come in next week, and things aren't quite ready for them yet.'

'It was good of you to take the time out today, then.'

'Not at all. You wanted to see L'Anse-aux-Meadows and I needed a day off. I'm glad we could work something out.'

It was such a belittling of the day that Prunella had earlier thought so radiant that she was suddenly on the edge of tears, and her, 'Goodbye, then,' had to fight its way out through a thick lump in her throat. When she got to her room she flung herself on the bed, burning with the ecstatic memory of their kiss and certain, at the same time, that somehow if only he hadn't kissed her things would still be all right.

CHAPTER FIVE

'You hadn't forgotten, had you?' Kathleen Kuusinen said to a blank-faced Prunella at seven o'clock the next evening.

Standing in the open doorway of her room, dressed in her oldest jeans and sweater, and with a towel around her neck and her hair still dripping from a fresh wash, Prunella could only be honest. 'Yes, I had.'

The Sunday evening video party at Kathleen's sister Deirdre's house. . .On Friday she had been looking forward to yesterday's picnic with Rourke, and since then his kiss and her regret had filled her thoughts. Tonight, after the early meal at the hospital dining-room, she had planned an evening in her room, and now here was Kathleen, cheerfully proposing to put her in the company of the very man she wanted to avoid.

Or was Kathleen so cheerful? Her face had shuttered over a little now, and Prunella wondered if she felt personally insulted at her new friend's forgetfulness.

'But of course I'll come,' she said quickly. 'I don't know how it came to go out of my head like that. I suppose because our arrangement wasn't really finalised on Thursday.'

'Yes, perhaps it's my fault,' Kathleen said. 'I should have phoned you to see if you were definite about it '

'No, I said I'd let you know and I didn't,' Prunella answered. She knew now why it had happened. In the back of her mind she had been expecting Rourke to mention the event, and when he hadn't. . .'Can you wait while I change and dry my hair?'

'Well, dry your hair, but there's no need to change,'

Kathleen said. 'It's a very casual evening, and you look fine.'

'No, but I don't feel fine.' She didn't say that to dress nicely would somehow be a defence against her feelings about Rourke.

'It's up to you, then.' Again, Kathleen was a little distant, and when Prunella told her to make herself at home her brisk look around the small bedsitter was rather forced in its cheerfulness.

Prunella switched on her blow-drier, then said above the noise, 'You look tired. Shall I make you a cup of tea?'

'No, we'll get plenty of that at Deirdre's,' she answered. 'But yes, I haven't slept too well these past couple of nights. My wrists feel good, and I can move my right hand beautifully now, but I feel stupid about the whole thing.'

Prunella switched off the blow-drier. 'Listen, you're bound to feel that way, especially if you're awake at three in the morning. No one else feels you're stupid, though. Your family and friends are just incredibly relieved that you're all right.'

'I know, and realising what it would have done to them if I'd. . .*succeeded*, I suppose is the word. . .will stop me from ever trying it again, no matter what happens.'

'You've got to give yourself time,' Prunella said. 'It's hard but sometimes time is the only answer, the only thing that will get certain feelings to go away.'

It was something she had been saying to herself all day as she relived Rourke's kiss time after painful time. . .But no, it wasn't the kiss that was painful to remember, it was the way Rourke had cut himself off from her afterwards, making a clear signal that any relationship between them based on that kiss was out of the question.

Spending tonight with him would be hard, but it did

have some positive value. She would be able to show him that he needed not fear any embarrassing scenes on her part. She had accepted that any spark he might have felt for her had flared briefly and died, and now she simply had to do as she had told Kathleen to do—wait until time dulled this uncomfortable sensation of rejection and loss.

While Kathleen sat on the edge of the bed, doodling idly on some scrap paper, Prunella slipped quickly into the purple jersey dress she had worn the other night, dried her hair till it framed her face in a fine halo of white gold and touched her eyes and lips with make-up. The hair could have been neater and the make-up less sketchy, but, as Kathleen had said, it was a casual evening.

'Ready!' she announced after fifteen busy minutes, then went over to the bed, adding curiously, 'What is it that you've drawn?'

Kathleen lifted her bandaged forearm from the page awkwardly. 'Oh, just whales.'

'Whales?'

'I always doodle whales, for some reason—whales and waves. This one's a minke, and this is a humpback, and this is a pilot.' She gestured with the pen that was still grasped a little awkwardly in her hand.

'But they're not just doodles, Kathleen, they're proper sketches. They're very good. I mean, your wrist is still in bandages.'

'Do you think so?' She shrugged dismissively, but Prunella detected an eagerness in her, as if the drawings were more important than she was letting on.

'Yes, I do think so,' she answered, then said no more about it, sensing that she should go slowly on this subject.

It was a fifteen-minute walk to Deirdre's, and when they got there, rosy-cheeked and tingling after the exer-

cise and the crisp night air, everyone else was gathered.
Quite a crowd, too, although it was all family.

Almost all. Glenda James was there, hanging eagerly
on the arm of a man who looked a lot like Rourke—
older, though, with sharper features and shallower eyes.

'My brother Finlay,' Kathleen said, and Prunella
smiled at him.

'Hi, gorgeous!' he said, then detached himself from
Glenda and went into the kitchen, where tea, coffee, beer
and fruit juice were being dispensed.

'I don't think much of this place, do you?' Glenda
whispered with a sibilant hiss. She wore a cheap party
dress with a black lace bodice and short white taffeta
skirt that could have used a more thorough ironing.

Prunella was at a loss, and answered, 'I've only just
arrived.' After three weeks of making no effort whatsoever to be friendly, was Glenda now taking her on as a
confidante?

'But look at this room. It hasn't been redecorated
since the house was built! This is going to be a real wow
of an evening. . .' Glenda's small mouth turned down
sarcastically.

'Prunella, this is Meg, a family friend,' Rourke said,
looming in front of her all at once. She hadn't thought it
possible that she would be glad to see him, but in fact
she was. It was better than having to find a response to
Glenda's petty comments. Rourke stood beside a short
woman of about thirty who wore her straight black hair
in a twenties-style bob with a heavy, glossy fringe. 'Meg,
meet Prunella Murdoch,' he went on, and they
exchanged some polite phrases.

Brown-eyed Meg was an executive secretary in
Toronto and was home in St Anthony for an extended
summer holiday between jobs. Prunella found her accent
hard to follow—it was a standard Canadian drawl which
slipped sometimes into very broad local vowels—and

their exchange was an effort. When the other woman moved away, guided by Rourke's hand on her elbow, and Prunella found herself alone for a moment, it was a relief.

Around her the atmosphere was lively and no one was bothering any more with formal introductions. An old woman with wiry grey hair sat in the place of honour— a large, faded green armchair in front of the television. She had reddened hands that were swollen from arthritis at each joint, her back was curved by osteoporosis, and her plain dress was covered by an apron as if she hadn't remembered to take it off after a day of housework. For a moment Prunella wondered who she was, then Kathleen went up to her, rested a bandaged left arm on the bent shoulder and gave her a warm kiss, and she realised with a shock that this must be Rourke's mother.

Her curiosity roused, she looked more carefully around the room and saw that Glenda's remarks, unkind and unnecessary though they were, were essentially acurate. The house was small and somewhat shabby, its knick-knacks and decorations cheap, mass-produced things, and the television and video player the only objects of value in the room. For the first time it came home to her that some members of Rourke's family were poor.

They certainly didn't seem unhappy, though. Seeing the laughter in the faces of Deirdre Rumbelow's children and the way they teased and cuddled their grandmother, Prunella could tell that this sprawling family was far more relaxed than her own arid set of relatives — indifferent stepfather, ineffectual mother, and spoiled young half-brother Duane.

'Katie, where's my darling little cousin Julia?' four-teen-year-old Stephanie Rumbelow called across the room.

Kathleen, orange juice in hand, replied, 'At home in

bed, as she should be, of course,' while Deirdre cut in
with,

'You know I can't have the whole family every time,
Steph. Once a year at Christmas is enough for a clan
this size. Conlan and Daphne and their lot can come
next time, and the Harriman gang and all those others
can find their own entertainment.'

Harriman. The name rang a bell, then it clicked just
as Alison Harriman herself came out of the kitchen
bringing a big bowl of crisps. The part-time switchboard
operator at the hospital was another one of Rourke's
older married sisters! Her curiosity last week made sense
now. Of course she felt some interest in someone who
might be Rourke's girlfriend.

Well, she needn't waste any more time on me,
Prunella said stoutly to herself.

'Can I find you a seat, fair lady?' said a voice close
beside her that was very like Rourke's. In fact, it was so
like Rourke's that she jumped and flushed as she turned
to face Finlay Donovan. He noticed her reaction and
looked pleased.

'Thank you,' she said quickly on as steady a note as
she could. She wondered where Glenda had got to, then
saw that her fellow nurse was hovering over the supper
table, eating with a steady concentration that contrasted
with her slighting remarks about the evening and the
décor.

Finlay helped Prunella courteously into a low chair,
then sat on its padded arm and toasted her with a large
gulp of wine. Was drinking a Donovan family problem?
she wondered uneasily. But no, Kathleen had orange juice
this evening, and so did Rourke and his two older sisters.
Their husbands Bill Rumbelow and Wilf Harriman had
beers, and old Mrs Donovan drank tea.

Finlay *had* been drinking too much, though. She was

enveloped in a cloud of fumes and hoped he would soon turn his attention back to Glenda.

'So,' he said, leaning towards her, 'how is a lovely lady like yourself settling down in our town?'

'Leave her alone, Fin,' Rourke growled, and perhaps his voice wasn't the same as Finlay's after all. It was slightly deeper and had a fuller sound. He stood threateningly beside his brother, who slid off the chair arm with a grin.

'I'm afraid I'm the black sheep of the family, Miss Murdoch.'

'Harmless enough, though,' Rourke said easily, giving him a casual shove. 'When are you going back to New York?'

'Well, I've sent out my résumé—as we say down there. . .' suddenly he was speaking in a classic American drawl '. . .so it's a matter of waiting till I get a few bites.'

'Finlay works on Wall Street,' Rourke said with a touch of irony.

'Although I'm not exactly a financier,' his older brother put in, 'just a corporate lackey. My last company—a Canadian concern—went bust in a big way a couple of months ago.'

'Still,' Prunella said, aware that there were undercurrents to this conversation that she did not understand, 'the whole family seem to have very diverse and interesting careers. What do the others do? You must all have had to work hard to get an education.'

There was an awkward pause, and Rourke's mouth set in a grim line, then Finlay said on a laugh 'Education? All of us? Ouslan and Marian can't read or write!'

'I must find Meg,' Rourke said abruptly. 'She'll want a seat. Deirdre's nearly ready to start the film.'

'It's a bit of a sore point within the family, as you might guess,' Finlay explained, once again leaning towards Prunella in a confidential way that she didn't really like. The more she looked and listened, the less like Rourke he seemed. 'The fact that one of us ended up an extremely well-paid surgeon, while most of the rest of us are floundering. Especially Conlan. You may wonder how that could happen. . .'

His tone implied that Rourke's success was not to his own credit, and Rourke himself had obviously been very uncomfortable about Finlay's revelation.

There are too many undercurrents in this family, Prunella thought to herself. Too many stories of failure and success and heartbreak.

She saw that Rourke and Meg had found chairs near to one another—not armchairs like the one she had sunk into, but stiff-backed dining chairs that allowed them to sit very close together. Meg laughed, and as she tossed her head that bobbed black hair swung like a glossy bell around her face. She seemed very happy in Rourke's company. His mood was less obviously positive, but as the video machine was turned on and the lights were turned out Prunella saw, with a burning tightness in her throat, that he had his arm around the girl's soft shoulders

'Must we have the clearing of the throat, Mr Scioto?' Rourke heard his own voice come out like vinegar, and would have bitten back the petty question if he could.

'I'm sorry, I've got a bit of an allergy,' the flustered medical student said. For some reason Rourke did find him intensely irritating, although he had already shown, during this first week of a nine-week rotation in St Anthony, that he had the makings of an excellent surgeon—probably in some esoteric specialty that didn't yet exist.

The operation—repair of an abdominal aortic aneurysm—proceeded, and Joseph Scioto cleared his throat again, then mumbled an apology that was even more irritating than the original offence had been.

What is the matter with me? Rourke wondered. Aloud, he said, 'Could you take over here, Dr Green?'

'Of course.' She stepped in with a slightly puzzled look on her face. The middle of a delicate procedure like this wasn't exactly the usual place for a surgeon to put his resident through her paces.

Rourke watched her as she sutured the tiny piece of grafted vessel and didn't need to say anything. It was careful, competent work, and it gave him the luxury of spending a moment with his own thoughts. Can I get her transferred to Theatre One for routine surgery hours? he wondered, and it was Prunella Murdoch he was thinking of, not Dr Karen Green. But they'd still be on call together from time to time for emergency work, and would still run into each other in the rooms and passages that serviced the two theatres, not to mention in the dining-room at mealtimes.

He moved away from the table a little and looked at her covertly as she stood beside Dr Green—neat, compact, composed, alert, absorbed in her work. He cursed himself for allowing her into the realm of his senses on Saturday when he had already made up his mind to squash the attraction he felt for her. Kissing her like that had not been part of the plan at all, and it was unfair to both of them.

The hot yellow lights over the operating table reminded him now of the way the sun's warmth had coaxed that sensual response from himself and her. And yet it hadn't only been the sun, nor the wine, for that matter. It was more the way they had enjoyed each other's company—which hadn't been part of the plan either. He had honestly hoped to find her boring, trivial, bitchy, obtuse. . .*anything* that he could have latched on to as an unbearable fault.

It was clear, then, that different tactics were called for. Simply discipline, perhaps. A man went through life being aware of many women. It was chance as much as anything else, Rourke believed, that brought a particular man and woman together to form a permanent relationship, and in this case he wasn't prepared to let chance have the final say. He simply wouldn't follow through on what had started to happen between Prunella and himself, and in time—probably quite a short time, if his relationship with Meg started to develop—he would wonder what he had ever seen in the girl.

Meg Slade. He wanted his future in St Anthony to lie with her. She was from here. She knew the place. She had it in her blood, as he did. Her father was a fisherman as his own had been, but she knew the city life of Toronto as well. She said that she was planning to return there in late September to take up a position as private secretary to an up-and-coming creative director in the world of advertising, but he wasn't convinced that her commitment to the city was a firm one. Spending over three months back here in St Anthony.. . . Didn't that indicate that she might be having second thoughts, rediscovering the importance of her origins, as he had done?

He had always liked Meg. She had been at school with his sister Fiona, now thirty, who taught high-school history in Yarmouth, Nova Scotia. This meant that he had known her, on and off, for. . .good heavens, it must be nearly twenty years.

He had a pretty good idea that there had been some fairly heavy involvements in her past, but then he was not exactly innocent of that sort of thing himself—during the years in Montreal when he had been looking so hard for the right direction in his life. As long as Meg was not carrying around any destructive emotional baggage from those past involvements, he would not regard them as a drawback.

A deeper part of himself was nagged at by the feeling that this was all too neat and cold-blooded, when the other major decisions in his life had come about in surges of emotion that could not be denied, but his surgeon's brain said that this was nonsense. Reasonless passion in affairs of the heart was for pimply adolescents and led either to heartbreak or embarrassment—neither of which particularly appealed to the man he now was.

And he was dwelling on the whole business far too much at the moment. It was the girl's fault. Prunella. He should never have kissed her, and he felt extremely bad about it. . .Which brought him right back to where he had started.

'That was beautifully done, Karen,' he said, rousing himself from the downward-spiralling pattern of thought. 'Your technique is really improving.'

Prunella felt the atmosphere in Theatre Two relax a little, and let out a controlled sigh herself. Dr Donovan seemed to be in a bad mood this Thursday morning. He had snapped at his new medical student, who was an eager, goggle-eyed young man with an irritating frog in his throat.

Poor Joseph Scioto! He looked as nervous as Prunella remembered feeling on her very first day in Theatre as a second-year student, and she made a mental note to say something cheerful to him during the break that would soon come before the next operation. No sense in the whole team's being on edge, or down in the dumps.

It hadn't been an easy week for her, but she was beginning to hope that the worst was over. Rourke had been distantly friendly, had frowned whenever he saw her coming, and hadn't mentioned either Saturday's picnic or Sunday's evening at Deirdre Rumbelow's.

Clearly her sense that their kiss had spoiled things was accurate.

She didn't blame him in any way. He had set out to be friendly, had gone a little further than his true feelings warranted, realised this, and was now keeping his distance. It was part of the pattern of courtship the world over. People made mistakes. If his kiss had had the opposite effect on her it wasn't really his fault and he must never know of it. The hard knot of hurt inside her would ease away with time.

And ironically she was feeling better about life in St Anthony now than she had two weeks ago, before she had met him. She and Eileen Simpson, the St John's nurse with whom she had had tea the day she had first met Rourke, had planned a visit to the Grenfell Museum this coming Saturday. It was dreadful that neither of them had been yet, when it was Sir Wilfred Grenfell who had started the medical service here in St Anthony amid such appalling conditions early this century—and Kathleen had invited her over to dinner next Tuesday night.

As long as Rourke Donovan did the decent thing and kept out of her way, and as long as Kathleen didn't talk about him too much, these uncomfortable feelings would settle down, even if they didn't quite disappear.

'Sutures, Nurse,' Dr Donovan said.

Quickly Prunella returned her attention to her work.

It must be Eileen, Prunella thought when the knock sounded on her door that evening.

She switched off the small cassette deck that had been playing a jazz-ballet exercise tape and pulled off the purple towelling sweat-band that had been keeping her fine spun-sugar hair off her face as she moved.

But it was Rourke Donovan who stood in the doorway, filling it with his capable frame in a way that Eileen, as petite as Prunella herself, could never have done. At

once Prunella was self-conscious. Her semi-sheer black
Lycra tights and purple leotard with its low back and
spaghetti straps had seemed decent enough for Eileen,
and it was easy to explain to a fellow female that she
was keeping her figure toned and in shape, but now that
it was Rourke. . .

The slippery stretch Lycra moulded itself to every
curve of her body, including neat, firm breasts, hourglass
waist and hips, and thighs that could perhaps have been
an inch or two slimmer. The neckline of the leotard
dipped down in a wide V, and Prunella knew that there
was a mist of sweat there, brought on by the first ten
minutes of energetic warm-up.

She darted quickly behind the bathroom door, pulled
a silky kimono off its hook and slid her arms into the
cool, heavy fall of its wide sleeves. It crossed in the front
and fastened with a wide black sash, and the bold
pattern of an Oriental-style dragon in sea-toned purples
and greens at least made a convincing match with her
work-out gear.

'I've come at a bad time,' Rourke said.

'Oh, no, I was just finishing,' she lied. The furniture
was pushed back to give extra room for jazz-ballet kicks
and wide-reaching floor work. Did he want to sit down?
'I can. . .' She gestured at the most comfortable chair, a
low one with arms and seat upholstered in blue grey
wool.

'Let me.' He crossed to it in three strides and pulled it
out from against the bed, but then refused to sit in it so
that she had no choice but to sink into its depths herself.

He chose for himself the stiff-backed wooden chair
that went with the small desk in the far corner of the
room, and sat on it backwards with his legs straddled to
either side and his arms folded on top of the back. It was
a defensive position, and one that said very clearly, I
haven't come here tonight to get close to you in any way.

'Can I get you a cup of tea?' she offered tentatively, feeling that politeness demanded it. Since she ate all her meals in the dining-room, tea and coffee was all the bed-sit was equipped to provide.

But he shook his head almost before she had finished speaking. He was dressed in dark tailored trousers and one of the white business shirts he usually wore when making rounds or taking Wednesday's out-patient clinic, and she wondered if he had come directly from work. It was after eight, but a surgeon had all sorts of reasons for haunting hospital corridors at odd hours.

'I'm not staying long,' he said. 'You go ahead, though, if you want one.'

'No, it's all right.' She wanted to tell him 'Say what you've come to say and have done with it!'—since this was clearly a visit he had keyed himself up for and felt quite uncomfortable about. He cleared his throat. 'Have you caught Joe Scioto's allergy?' she quipped drily.

'What? Oh! Did I. . .? Sorry.'

'Don't worry, I was only joking.'

'Prunella, I have to apologise for Saturday,' he said suddenly, leaving the chair in one fluid movement and taking a pace so that he was half turned away from her.

'No, you don't,' she answered evenly.

'But I do. It was unfair. It shouldn't have happened.'

'Is that why you've come tonight?'

He hesitated, then turned towards her again and answered, 'Yes, if you want to be blunt.'

'Then I wish you hadn't. It wasn't necessary. These mistakes. . .happen between people.'

'You really feel that?'

'Yes, I do.' It was hard to say, but it was the truth.

His craggy features softened suddenly with what must be relief. He had obviously been afraid of recrimination, tears, a scene. When he spoke again, after studying her for a long moment so that her gaze faltered before his,

his tone was gentle and thoughtful. 'You're an unusual woman, Prunella Murdoch.'

'Am I?' She forced a light laugh. 'I don't think so.'

It seemed like a good moment to pull herself up out of the chair, as a signal to him that she regarded their exchange as completed. But the long kimono had somehow got caught beneath one of the chair legs, and it pulled her back so that she went off balance. Immediately he was beside her, and his strong fingers on her upper arm steadied her as he lifted the front of the chair with his other hand and set her free.

She hated the fact that they had been forced to touch. The warmth of him quickly penetrated the thin silk of the kimono and she could see his chest, almost level with her eyes, rising and falling with his breathing. Worst of all, she could smell the faint musky aura of maleness and woodsy aftershave that hovered around him, and it brought Saturday's kiss back to her far too powerfully.

He released her as soon as she was safely on her feet, dropping her arm as if deeply embarrassed at the contact, then he backed towards the door. Good! He was going! There was to be no pretence. She held the door open for him and he stepped out into the hallway, then, before she could wish him a polite goodnight, he suddenly pressed his fingers to his lips and touched the fingers to her forehead.

'Take care of yourself, Prue,' he said softly

At that her control broke, and words came tumbling out on a low, vibrating pitch. 'You shouldn't have come—you really shouldn't. You've made things worse now. I wasn't angry before. Or upset.' Not quite the truth. 'Now I'm both. Couldn't you see that it was the wrong thing to do?'

'Prunella, I——'

'Go. Don't make it worse. There's nothing left to say.'

'But we're going to have to meet——'

'Of course,' she cut him off. 'And we'll both be very civilised about it, whether we meet at the hospital or anywhere else. I'm sure we'd even be capable of going out together, as long as neither Saturday nor, even more importantly, this ridiculous scene are ever referred to again.'

'If that's what you want. . .'

'It is. Don't forget it, please.'

'I won't, Prunella Murdoch. Believe me, I won't.' His face had frozen over now and he spoke through tight lips. His eyes had narrowed—in shock or anger, she didn't know which—so that they looked, not for the first time, like the eyes of a wolf on the prowl.

When he had disappeared down the corridor, when she could no longer hear his crisp tread descending the stairs, when she managed to control her trembling enough to move, Prunella went back into her room and closed the door.

She didn't finish her jazz work-out that night.

CHAPTER SIX

THE clouds were like fluffy, freshly washed sheep grazing in a flat blue meadow. From this height, the sea was just a wrinkled cloth—impossible to believe that those white ruffles betokened strong-muscled waves metres high. Then Prunella saw something else—irregular shapes where the blue cloth ended, giving way to sand and rock, and finally meadows and forests.

'Where are we?' she asked Greg Mead, having to raise her voice a little above the noise of the nine-seat Aerocommander aircraft.

'The big island beneath us now is Fogo,' he answered, 'and out to the left you can start to see the Wadham Islands. Beyond is the mainland.'

'Yet that's water I can still see glinting in the sun, isn't it?'

'Yes. Those are ponds. You don't realise quite how much of Newfoundland is covered by lakes and ponds until you see it from the air.'

'And is that the last we'll see of the ocean?'

'Of the Atlantic proper, yes. But we'll cross Trinity Bay and Conception Bay as we approach St John's.'

It was Prunella's first official flight, and as easy a one as she could have hoped for. She had signed up for the short training course as soon as her three months in St Anthony made her eligible to do so, and had learnt about such things as oxygen equipment, setting up intravenous lines while in flgiht, and some detail on the way the Medevac system worked.

Now it was her first weekend rostered on, and she was spending this sunny Sunday afternoon escorting a sev-

enty-three-year-old fisherman to St John's. It seemed
more like a joy-ride than work that earned excellent
overtime rates. Ernie Cull was a good patient and
seemed almost to be looking forward to his stay in
hospital in St John's, although he was about to commence a course of radiation treatment for prostate cancer
there.

'I've never even been as far as Corner Brook before,'
he had said to Prunella. 'And that's only five hundred
kilometres, like.'

Greg Mead was using the flight, as staff were permit-
ted to do when there was space, as the first leg of a two-
week holiday trip to Florida. Also on board were Rob
and Beth Miller, parents of a baby born prematurely ten
weeks earlier.

Tiny Lindsay Jane had been born in St Anthony and
had experienced *her* first medical flight when less than a
day old. A neonatal care team had flown from the
Janeway Hospital to St Anthony to collect her and
transport her in safety, and during her weeks in St John's
she had slowly, and with several setbacks and surgery to
correct a heart defect, gained strength and weight until
she had reached the required five pounds. Prunella
would be on hand as a medical escort for the return
flight, but it was purely a routine safety precaution, and
the baby's parents would soon experience the familiar
reality of disturbed nights and frequent laundering.

Old Ernie Cull shifted in his stretcher and made a
sound that was half-grunt, half-cry.

'Are you all right there, Mr Cull?' Prunella said,
leaning towards him from the seat she was belted into.

'I'm all right, yes,' he nodded cautiously, then added,
'but I wish we wasn't going over the land, like.'

'Why is that, Mr Cull?'

'I like going over the sea better. If we had trouble

with the plane, like, and had to come down on the water, it'd only be like going over in a boat, now, wouldn't it?'

'Probably,' Prunella agreed carefully.

'Well, I've been over in a boat half a dozen times, had to swim or wait for my mates to pull me out. I remember jigging for cod once out of. . .'

The anecdote continued for some time and was rather rambling, but brought a vivid picture, none the less, of Ernie Cull as a likely lad of sixteen moving nimbly about a small dinghy, and Prunella felt a little sad for a moment. Ernie was so stiff and rheumatic now that he could scarcely walk, and the way of life he knew in his prime, years before St Anthony was linked to the outside world by road, had drastically changed. She remembered how she had overheard Rourke Donovan talking to Dr Green one day about the government programme in the 1960s to resettle people from the most isolated 'outports' into larger centres.

'The resettlement destroyed something,' he had said. 'Perhaps it's only hindsight that makes it seem such an obvious mistake. Or perhaps that old outport way of life was doomed anyway, but it makes me angry and sad, all the same.'

Rourke. . . It was nearly three months, now, since the night he had come to her apartment, and his departure then had turned out to be as final as it had seemed. They met very frequently, of course. Almost daily, in fact, because if they didn't see each other in surgery they were bound to meet in the car park, in the dining-room, or at some Donovan family event.

Through Kathleen Prunella had become very involved with the sprawling Donovan clan. She had met them all now. The twins, Dermot and Devlin, were quiet, easy-going men, content with their work as fishermen. Fiona, who came for two weeks summer holiday, was bright and pleasant and newly engaged to be married to a man

in Yarmouth, Nova Scotia, where she had settled.
Deirdre and Alison were women in their early forties,
whose concerns centred on their husbands and children.
Marian was very like her mother—reserved, tough, with
qualities of strength and simplicity that belonged to an
earlier era of Newfoundland life.

Finlay seemed to have finished with Glenda James,
and had made it clear more than once that he would be
happy to have Prunella as a replacement, but she had
politely frosted his advances. I'm not going to be hurt
by *two* Donovan men, she said to herself, although in
fact she felt no attraction towards Finlay at all. A little
strange, perhaps, when he looked so much like Rourke.

And then there was Conlan. Sixteen years older than
Rourke, he could almost have been his father. Once
they, too, might have been similar in looks, but the
harsher and more physical life Conlan had led, and the
fact that in his early childhood nutrition in the island—
not even a part of Canada at that stage—was poor, had
taken its toll.

He was shorter than Rourke, stockier, and slightly
stooping now. He looked older than his forty-eight years,
and it was clear that he was not content with his life
as a fisherman, as the twins were. The sea had buffeted
his face into heavy creases, but his eyes—very like
Kathleen's—were a piercing blue in that leathery face.

To Prunella he was gruffly friendly, and she still didn't
understand the source of his enmity with Rourke. The
Donovan family seemed to step around it without bringing it into the open. When there was a family gathering
one of the two brothers would always be invited, but
never both.

As for Rourke, he was also friendly with Prunella and
she with him. In fact they were so polite about it all that
she was amazed no one else seemed to notice the falsity
of it. Sometimes she felt her face would crack from

smiling in his presence, and she could have laughed at
their utterly correct exchanges:

'Nice to see you here, Prunella.'

'Yes, it's a glorious day for berry-picking and a
barbecue, isn't it?'

'Do you plan on swimming too?'

'Yes, I brought my costume. Kathleen says I'll find
these ponds cold, but Inverness isn't exactly in the
tropics, so I think I'll manage.'

'I'm sure you will.'

'And is Meg coming today?'

'Yes. She had to help her parents with something this
morning, but she'll be here later on.'

'It'll be nice to see her.'

Nice, nice, nice! Meg too was very nice, and if she
knew or suspected that there had once, very briefly, been
something more between Prunella and Rourke than
these polite, empty phrases she didn't show it. But, after
all, why should she? It was she who was undisputably
the woman in Rourke's life now. There was no need for
jealousy or pettiness.

Now Prunella wondered what would happen when
Meg returned to Toronto. The summer had come to an
end, the days were closing in, and she was due to leave
for her new secretarial job in just a few days' time.
Would her departure precipitate an engagement? A
deadline like that often did. And Rourke had been
looking unhappy lately, as if he didn't want Meg to go.
There was a look he wore that Prunella recognised now:
he would bite his lower lip and jut his chin outward
more forcefully. He would get a distant look in his eye,
and when someone spoke to him he would frown and
narrow his eyes before he replied.

No one else seemed to have noticed these signs of
unhappiness, though.

'Rourke's doing so well here in St Anthony,' Kathleen

said more than once. 'I never thought he'd settle here
again, but it seems so right for him now. I don't know
what's happening with him and Meg, but. . .we'll see.'

Kathleen herself had had some black times over the
summer and was still adrift as far as future plans went,
but looking after Conlan's youngest two children each
day seemed to provide her with a degree of focus and
contentment.

And me? Prunella wondered, idly watching the landscape unfold below her like a child's map—toy houses,
bridges, boats and trees.

Mr Cull was asleep now. Greg Mead had his nose
buried in a spy thriller, and the Millers were studying a
department-store catalogue and talking about curtains
for the baby's room. She had the leisure to think about
her life and to wonder about her future. It was something
she tried not to do too often.

Actually, she was happier here than she would have
thought possible three months ago. The work was fascinating, Eileen was a good friend among the nursing staff,
and her room now had welcoming touches of her own
personality. Spending time outdoors at the height of
Newfoundland's short, vibrant summer had been zestful,
and now she was looking forward to the winter sports
that Newfoundlanders themselves felt more at home
with—cross-country skiing, and riding the snow-mobiles
that had replaced the old dog-driven *komatiks* or sleds.

She wasn't breaking her heart over Rourke Donovan
either. It required will-power, but she had plenty of that.
In a few more months she would be able to think of him
simply as her senior in surgery, Kathleen's brother, and
in all likelihood Meg Slade's fiancé.

Did she want to stay in St Anthony another year,
though? Recruitment of nursing staff was a long process,
and she had been asked, along with everyone else, to
indicate as soon as possible whether she wanted to

extend her contract. At the moment, though, she just didn't know. Did it depend on Rourke? She told herself that it didn't, but a voice deeper inside told her naggingly that this was not the truth.

The boats in Conception Bay looked bigger beneath the plane now, and she realised that they were losing height. Ten minutes later they had landed in St John's, where an ambulance waited on the Tarmac to continue Ernie Cull's journey to the hospital. The ambulance had also brought Lindsay Jane Miller to meet the plane, and her parents gave her an emotional greeting. With an older child at home, they had only been able to make one visit to her during her long stay in hospital.

'She looks beautiful,' Greg Mead said. He had been on hand at her birth, had been an important factor in her survival, and had escorted her by ambulance to meet the Janeway Hospital team at the airstrip when she had been flown out to St John's. 'Although I think she has less hair.'

'But look at the colour of it now!' the happy father said. Little Lindsay had been born with a fine dark crop of hair, which she had soon lost. Now new hair was coming in and it was golden, lying flat on her tiny head like a shining cap. Even Ernie Cull wanted to look at her, and refused to depart in the ambulance until he had done so.

The turn around, which included refuelling and an engine check, was soon completed, Greg Mead left amid good wishes for his holiday, and they were ready to take off again. The weather on the return trip was just as beautiful as it had been on the way out, and by early afternoon they were approaching the northern peninsula again, with the wide expanse of the Atlantic Ocean stretching on the right-hand side of the plane.

There were no icebergs drifting in the Labrador current today. It was too late in the season for those now. Prunella wondered if Rourke had found an opportunity over the summer to hitch a ride on one of the routine flights in order to fulfil his ambition. She sensed that it was not something he would have told her about if he had. That Saturday picnic trip to L'Anse-aux-Meadows, including anything they had talked about that day, was one subject that never came up between them in all those light chats they had.

Don't think about that, she told herself sternly, and began very deliberately to plan the rest of her day instead—a brisk walk out to the point, perhaps, followed by her jazz-ballet work-out, dinner in the dining-room with Eileen and several others, and then an evening of arranging the summer's photos in the two albums she had recently bought. There were several photos in which Rourke appeared, but she wouldn't look too closely at those. . .

'Hang on,' the pilot said. 'This is a radio call from Harbour Deep. Must be something up.'

A local St Anthony man, he had piloted aircraft in routine medical flights as well as emergencies for many years, and his calm words gave no hint of the fact that this could be something urgent. Since the message from Harbour Deep came only through Ross Kelland's earphones, and those of the co-pilot beside him, Prunella could only guess what was going on, although she listened intently to the pilot's words in reply.

'Yes, we're pretty well in the area. You've spoken with Base, of course. . .We can be on the ground within fifteen minutes—over. . .No, we have no doctor on board. . .' Then after a longer pause to listen, 'OK, we're on our way.' Only then did he raise his voice to address the others. 'Been an accident at Harbour Deep,' he said. 'We're going to pick him up. Prunella, get your headphones on and stand by for some instructions from Base.'

Prunella had to wait for several minutes before the message came through. She knew that Ross Kelland had probably been told more about the accident than he had revealed, since there were passengers on board the aircraft. It was hard not to busy her mind with useless speculations as she waited. A road accident? Unlikely. Harbour Deep was a very isolated outport, still without a connecting road to the outside world. It probably contained a few work vehicles for local use, that was all. If it wasn't a road trauma then it could well be something quite outside her range of experience.

Then she heard the voice of one of St Anthony's radio operators crackling in her ear. They exchanged the standard call-sign information, then he said, 'Stand by for Dr Donovan,' and a moment later came Rourke's voice.

'It's a sawmilling accident, Nurse,' he said, his voice clipped and a little distorted by static. 'The patient fell on to a circular saw. Left leg almost cut through at mid-thigh. The estimate is ninety per cent severed, and we're assuming amputation at this stage. We're going to do a helicopter transfer from the airstrip to the hospital, though, and, if there's any chance we can save the leg, we will. So I'll want your assessment.'

Prunella felt her adrenalin levels mounting as Rourke went on running through what he expected her to do while in flight with the patient. Her final, 'Over,' was calm but a little breathless, and she knew that the pressure would be on her next time she spoke with Rourke. She wondered, though, if he even knew who she was. A number of nurses did Medevac work. Today was her first shift, and perhaps he hadn't caught up with the fact that she had signed up for these extra hours.

Harbour Deep was a small community whose health centre was staffed by a single nurse. By necessity resourceful and independent, she spent, along with

nurses at a dozen of these health centres scattered over
the whole of northern Newfoundland and Labrador,
considerable periods of time alone and had to become
unusually skilled at diagnosis. These days scheduled
conferences by radio-telephone with medical staff at
Curtis Hospital made the work a lot easier and less
solitary, but when something like today's accident
occurred the old skills of the pioneer nurse in the days of
dog-sleds and kerosene lamps were called out.

Joan Jessop was in her late fifties now, and had held
several different posts in the Grenfell Mission system.
She was calm as she stepped forward on the windy
airstrip to greet Prunella, a strand of greying hair
escaping from her severe French roll to blow across her
face.

'One of the femoral arteries is severed,' she reported,
'and he's losing a lot of blood. They pressed a towel in
there as soon as it happened. I've cleaned around that
and packed gauze in there to stem the bleeding more.
Keep your eye on it. One IV so far, but you'll want to
put in a couple more. Ice. Sedative, orally. Dr Donovan
may want you to give something through the IV. It's
still only twenty-five minutes since it happened. The
fluid is the urgent thing.'

The pilot and co-pilot were loading the stretcher into
the back of the plane while the two nurses spoke
together.

'Dr Donovan wonders if it can be saved,' Prunella
said.

'I doubt it.' The older woman shook her head. 'I
haven't had time to think about it, but I'm assuming an
amputation, and that's what I've told his wife. She
insisted on knowing the truth. If there's better news later
on, well and good.'

'Is his wife coming?'

'No.' Joan Jessop's face fell and she shook her head.

'She has a baby due in eight weeks. She's with family now, but I must get back to her.'

'Of course.'

'She's in a worse state than he is at the moment, and that's not good.'

'Goodness, no!' A pregnant wife! It was an awful situation, but there was no time to discuss that side of it now.

Prunella boarded the small plane again, remembering what she had been told about approaching it while the propellers were moving. She had everything already prepared for setting up an IV and knew it was urgent that she do so. With difficulty she found a large vein in the patient's left arm. 'Clench your fist,' she ordered.

'All right.' He seemed dazed and remote, as if shrouded in cotton wool, emotion suppressed by shock as well as by the sedative Sister Jessop had given him.

'OK, here we go. This'll pinch a bit.' Please let it go in the first time, she prayed inwardly. At first she thought that the cannula *hadn't* gone in, but then she saw that it had, and started the solution flowing immediately at the most rapid rate possible. Next she did the same with a third IV in the thigh of the uninjured leg.

The plane was not even off the ground yet. Taking a second to look up, she could see Joan Jessop at the edge of the landing strip still watching the plane, her sturdy legs clad in thick stockings and solid brown leather shoes. In her early days in the region over thirty-five years ago she would have known people who had worked with Sir Wilfred Grenfell, would have been part of the successful campaign to wipe out tuberculosis here during the 1950s and 60s, would have seen some of the almost legendary improvisations of equipment and procedure. The Harbour Deep nurse turned to leave the airstrip, and Prunella lost sight of her as the plane began to gather speed.

She barely noticed when it left the ground. The patient, a man of about thirty-five named Lewis Moody, had to be hooked up to an EKG monitor. Talking to him and calming him was vital, and she needed to take temperature, blood-pressure and pulse readings, and report to Dr Donovan as soon as possible on the patient's condition.

He was waiting impatiently for the call and she could hear in his voice that he was determined to save the leg. 'Any warmth, though? Any warmth or pulse at all in the foot? Over.'

'I haven't had time to check yet—over,' she answered, not adding that she was reluctant to disturb the leg in any way. Joan Jessop's work in stopping the arterial blood flow was so hastily improvised that she was afraid it might not hold. She had already reported to Rourke that the patient's vital signs were stable and that his EKG showed a normal sinus rhythm.

'It's packed in ice? Over.'

'Yes, and I'm hesitant about. . .' She paused.

'No, all right. Leave it alone.' He came in quickly, disregarding proper call procedure. 'We'll carry on as if there's a chance.' He went on to instruct her about administering another sedative, and it seemed like only seconds after she had done this that they were skimming low over the bleak terrain that surrounded the St Anthony airstrip, on the point of landing.

She had almost forgotten Mr and Mrs Miller and their tiny baby. The couple had remained in their seats, with the baby strapped beside them in a travelling capsule. The infant herself had slept through the flight, and Prunella wondered if Lewis Moody was even aware that there was a baby on board. This was an ordeal for him, and if shock was protecting him from the pain, so much the better.

'Where's Minnie?' he asked at one point. His skin was

pale and damp, and there were dried spatterings of blood in his hair and on his forehead. Prunella had time now to take a gauze pad and wipe them away.

'Sister Jessop is with her,' she soothed at the same time. 'She'll report by radio regularly.'

She didn't want to say that he would be in surgery and would know nothing of what the health-centre nurse had to say about his wife's condition. But his thoughts had led in this direction themselves. 'My operation. How long will I be under?'

'Under anaesthesia?'

'Yes.'

'That depends. . .' On whether the leg can be saved, Prunella added to herself.

'As soon as I'm awake again. . .'

'You'll be given all the news of your wife. Please don't worry. She's in excellent hands.'

'I know that better than you do, I reckon,' he joked feebly, focusing on her for the first time. 'Joan's been at Harbour Deep for sixteen years now, and before that she was at Mary's Harbour for fifteen, and Port Saunders for seven. Minnie was born near Port Saunders and Joan delivered her.'

'That's wonderful, isn't it? She's an old friend, then,' Prunella smiled. 'But don't tire yourself by talking. . .' She continued to speak soothingly.

The plane taxied to a halt and the engine noise began to die down. Soon its sound was overtaken by the rougher rhythm of a helicopter, and when the plane's doors were opened two men already stood there, waiting to transport the stretcher. The Millers were being met by car and there was no time for Prunella to do more than fling her best wishes to them over her shoulder.

She held the IV bag up and had to run to keep it in position as they crossed the windswept space between the plane and the chopper. The day, although sunny, was chilly, and, with only thin beige stockings on her legs and a blue cotton uniform and light navy cardigan on the rest of her, Prunella was at once covered in goose-bumps.

The blast of air from the chopper's blades blew her hair into a wild frenzy and her ears rang once she was seated in the insect-like machine. A helicopter journey between the airstrip and the hospital was a rarity, she knew. In winter, weather too often made it too dangerous for this less stable form of flight, and usually a forty-five-minute drive by ambulance was the fastest way to accomplish the trip. In this case, however, every minute could make a difference to the future of Lewis Moody's leg, and Rourke had taken advantage of the fact that the helicopter was in the area.

The flight—Prunella's first by chopper—was swoop-ing and swift, but it was like a car going too fast and too smoothly on a winding road. In other words, it made Prunella feel distinctly queasy, and only the fact that she was continuing to monitor the patient closely kept her from a state of sheer misery.

Once they landed, a blessed five minutes later, her part in the drama was over. Rourke and the rest of the surgical team—including an Irish woman, Maureen O'Shaunessy, as scrub—would be standing by. Another team from Casualty met the chopper at its landing pad and would immediately cross-match the patient's blood ready for transfusion, which Prunella was fairly sure would be necessary. In the meantime more fluids would be given and possibly the 'universal' blood type, O negative.

In a whirlwind minute, therefore, she had given her patient into other hands and had only to take care of some follow-up paperwork before she was free to go home. She found the transition too sudden. A veteran of many surgical emergencies over the past two and a half years, she was used to being on the receiving end of these casualties, and she couldn't help going over the whole thing in her mind as she slowly removed her uniform in the silence of the bed-sitting-room.

By now Rourke will know if there's a chance of saving the leg. Then later, as she lay soaking in a hot bath, If it's amputation it would be over now. And later still, over dinner in a dining-room that seemed unusually empty tonight, If it's difficult surgery they're probably still going.

Fifteen minutes later, as she sat over a cup of tea, hoping that Eileen or another very pleasant girl, Rosalyn Jones, would come in, she saw the weary team in the doorway, several of them still in scrubs with white coats flung hastily on top. It made quite a crowd—Karen Green, Joseph Scioto, Alan Kerson and the orthopaedic resident who was under his wing at the moment on temporary rotation. Then that tall slightly round-shouldered man just behind Dr Green was Joel Nathan, the anaesthetist on call today. Maureen O'Shaunessy and Barbara McKay followed closely behind, and Prunella expected that one of them would respond to her wave and come over to give a report. But they weren't looking in her direction and didn't see her slight figure standing up near the windows.

Instead it was the last person to enter the large room who surveyed it, caught sight of her and came straight over—Rourke Donovan, still in the green cotton suit and soft-soled shoes he had worn during surgery.

'I thought you'd want to hear how it went,' he said, falling into a chair beside her. He looked tired, and the shadow of stubble that covered his jaw and chin by the end of a long day seemed unusually dark, but there was a satisfaction in his bearing too. His broad shoulders were relaxed and he looked ready for a hearty meal.

'You saved the leg,' she said.

'Someone's already told you. . .'

'No, I guessed. You would have looked different if you'd had bad news.'

'You're too observant for your own good, girl.'

'A scrub nurse has to learn to read a surgeon's every expression or her life would be hell.'

'So there's a textbook on it, is there?'

'Yes—*Surgical Body Language*, it's called, and it's six hundred pages long,' she retorted lightly. It was the most relaxed conversation they had had for three months. He must be extremely pleased with Lewis Moody's prognosis.

As if to answer this assumption, he said, 'It's too early to be completely sure, of course. When I first looked at it I thought it wasn't even worth trying, but once we had the mess cleared away we could see that there was some blood supply still reaching the foot. Alan put a plate on the leg bone. That was cut clean through, a beautiful neat slice, so there should be no problem there. We had to rejoin the sciatic nerve, clean out the femoral artery and rejoin it, re-attach the muscles.'

'What about infection? You must have——'

'Yes,' he nodded, anticipating her question. 'Very large doses of antibiotic over the next two weeks, and we've given anti-tetanus serum too, of course.'

'How soon will you know for certain if it's all right?'

'Within a few days we'll know if the leg is saved. How completely we've restored its function we won't know for months. Not till he's out of plaster and into some pretty intensive physiotherapy. You did good work, Prue.'

'Me?' She was very surprised, not being certain until just now that he had even known it was her on the other end of that radio hook-up. 'I didn't do anything! Joan Jessop——'

'Of course, and Alan Kerson, and Joel Nathan and little Miss O'Shaunessy and myself, but the fact that there were a lot of other people involved doesn't belittle your contribution. I heard it was your first flight today.'

'Yes,' she admitted. 'Quite an introduction! But don't forget I've done trauma work in Scotland.'

'All right,' he sighed, exaggerating his impatience, 'I can see you're going to refuse to take any credit at all. If you insist, it's all in a day's work and you did no more to save that leg than the man who sweeps the floor of the factory where they made the plane.'

'He probably finds it a very uplifting career,' she returned on a laugh. 'Yes, all right, thank you, Rourke. If you want to parcel out credit I'm happy to take my share. It's good to know the leg has a fighting chance.'

She expected him to return to his colleagues, who had gathered in a loud, newly relaxed group at one of the tables on the opposite side of the room, but he made no move to leave. For a minute there was an awkward silence, and Prunella started to wonder if she should get up instead, but then he spoke.

'Well, we've probably seen the last of the mild weather,' he said.

Weather? If that was all he had to talk about, why on earth didn't he go? Was he afraid she would think he was rude?

'I'm quite looking forward to the change,' she answered evenly, as if the topic were quite acceptable, if not precisely fascinating. 'I've never seen the ocean frozen before.'

'We'll have to go out in my snow-mobile,' he said casually. 'But the real snow doesn't come until December, and that's more than two months away yet.' He paused and then added even more casually than before, 'In the meantime. . .would you like to come whale-watching with me next Saturday?'

CHAPTER SEVEN

'SEE, you can tell he's a minke by his dorsal fin. It points backwards more sharply than the other species. Also he's the smallest,' Kathleen Kuusinen said. 'And of course he has a rhyming name. He's called Blinky the Minke.'

'He's gorgeous, Katie,' Prunella said.

This was a moment she had been waiting for all summer. She knew, although they never spoke openly about it, that Kathleen had been drawing and painting more and more as her wrists healed. The evidence lay in ink- or water-colour-stained fingers, in a pile of papers hastily pushed into a drawer one day when Prunella had been visiting Kathleen at her mother's house, and in a look of concentration she sometimes wore when looking at a particular feature of the landscape.

Today the two women were at Conlan's, looking after the youngsters Julia and Peter, and the three-year-old boy had unwittingly opened the door to Kathleen's secret with a round-eyed pleading that she 'draw more of the whale story'.

'Yes, whale story, whale story!' five-year-old Julia chanted. She jumped up and down eagerly and showed no sign of the stomach upset that had kept her home from her new school today. 'Did you bring all the pages so far?'

'Yes, I brought all the pages so far,' Kathleen replied with an air of weary resignation that couldn't fully disguise an eagerness to show Prunella what she had done.

Her cheeks were pink as she brought out the tidy

folder filled with sheets of drawing paper and pages of typed text. 'I started telling Julia and Peter about Blinky the Minke over summer,' she explained, 'just drawing pictures and making up the story as I went along. At first it was just fun for them; then I began to take it more seriously and I wondered if a publisher might be interested. Mrs Penfield at the library helped me to get a list of children's publishers, and I sent off some sample sketches and the text of the first story about six weeks ago. Yesterday I got a letter saying that they're very interested and they'd like to see the rest of the artwork.'

'And it's going to be a book, and she made it up for *us*!' Julia put in proudly.

'That's fabulous, Katie!'

'Adults might think it's a pretty silly story. A whale who helps ships and fellow sea-creatures and sends SOS messages by flashing the white patches on his flippers.'

'No, it's a delightful idea,' Prunella assured her. 'And the illustrations are gorgeous.'

The soft water-colours and more dramatic charcoal combined to suggest the unique land- and seascapes of Newfoundland, and Prunella thought that only a Newfoundlander born and bred could truly have captured the feeling of the place as Kathleen had done. At the same time, though, Kathleen's ability to identify with a child's perception of the world gave the drawings a flavour of magic and excitement.

'I thought it could be a series,' Kathleen was saying now, 'and I started having some other ideas as well. Maybe some stories set on the land. Bruce the Moose and his sister Lucy. Would that be too silly?'

'I don't think so, if you do it with the same spirit and love that you've put into the Blinky story.'

'Peter and Julia are the acid test,' Kathleen said. 'If they don't like something, I rethink.'

'But we like *everything*!' Julia said.

The whistling of the kettle punctuated her words, and Kathleen got up from the kitchen table where they had been sitting and began to make tea. It was a very homey kitchen, although it was obvious that, of all the Donovan clan, Conlan, his wife Daphne and large family of children had the biggest struggle to make ends meet.

Prunella had spent several afternoons here with Kathleen and the children over the summer, and she wondered, not for the first time, what it was that had driven such a wedge between Conlan and Rourke. With the fatalism about relationships that a large family often had, everyone seemed to accept that they would 'just never get on', but Prunella felt that there was a bitter hurt inside Rourke about the thing that should be healed if possible.

With a click of toenails, Drifter padded into the room and greeted Prunella, responding to the rough pats she gave him by sticking out his big pink tongue and panting noisily. Then he answered the children's cries of 'Here, boy, here, Drifter!' and the three of them went outside to play with an old tennis ball.

The dog was fully grown now, still a young animal but no longer a puppy at all. His paw was fully healed, of course. Prunella wondered if Conlan knew who had rescued his dog that day, but decided not to ask Kathleen about it. Instead she said, 'Have you told Rourke about the book, and shown the drawings to him?'

Katie turned away from the teapot, to which she had added what seemed to Prunella like a lethal quantity of tea. 'No, not yet. He's been pretty busy over the past week or two. Meg left for Toronto last Saturday, so of course they wanted to spend time together before she went.'

'Last Saturday?' Prunella echoed blankly, a sudden hollow opening in the pit of her stomach. It was the following day, Sunday, that Rourke had asked her to go

whale-watching with him. That outing was scheduled
for tomorrow, and, although she had been telling herself
all week that it was nothing to look forward to, she had
been doing so all the same.

It had coloured her mood today as well, adding an
extra nuance to the interest she felt in Kathleen's whale
story and making her study Blinky the Minke's shape
with special attention so that tomorrow she might be
able to surprise Rourke by the expertise of her
identification.

It serves me right for being so spineless, she said to
herself. I ought to have had more pride. I simply agreed
to go out with him as soon as he asked me. I might have
guessed he just wanted to fill in the hole that Meg left
when she went. It would have been more decent of him
if he'd at least waited a week or two! But what was
Kathleen saying?

'I'm not sure what's happening between those two,'
she mused, struggling over a tin of biscuits whose lid
would not come off. She waved away Prunella's
abstracted offer of help. 'Some heavy negotiations, I'd
say. I won't be surprised if Rourke leaves the hospital
and moves to Toronto.'

'And marries Meg?'

'Probably. We were all surprised when he took the job
here in the first place. And even more surprised when it
seemed to suit him. Now. . .who knows? No one quite
understands Rourke.'

'Does Meg?'

'Presumably. We'll just have to wait and see. Rourke's
the kind of man who doesn't tell his family he's going to
do a thing until three weeks after he's done it. . .
Although he did say last week that he'd be moving into
the house this weekend. I'll wait till he invites me round
and I'll bring the drawings with me and tell him then.'

The flush of excitement reappeared in her cheeks, and

Prunella surrendered her own emotional state for the sake of discussing Kathleen's writing plans in more detail. What was there to mull over, anyway? It was quite simple. Rourke was using her somehow to sort something out in his relationship with Meg. The outing tomorrow—and perhaps he had even forgotten about it—was at best a friendly gesture.

I'll go, Prunella decided. But I'll keep my distance.

Rourke was dressed for a day of cold wind and bitter salt spray. Prunella had no match in her wardrobe for his thick cream Aran sweater and heavy oilskin trousers and jacket. A stylish winter wool coat of royal blue wouldn't be right at all.

He saw her expression of dismay as he stood in the doorway of her bed-sit. 'Hadn't forgotten, had you?' One corner of his mouth rose in a half-smile.

'No, but I thought you might have,' she blurted, uncomfortably. A resolution to keep her distance was all very well, but when he stood there in the flesh, looking down at her like that, it threw her equilibrium to the four winds.

'Why on earth would I forget?' he said.

'Katie said you were moving into your house this weekend.'

'Well, not the whole time,' he growled. 'So let's get going, shall we?'

'I don't have the right clothes,' she said. 'That's why I looked doubtful just now. If it's cold maybe we shouldn't go after all.'

'Do you want to go?' he asked directly, his eyes narrowed and searching suddenly.

'I'd love to see whales,' she prevaricated.

He took it as a yes. 'I have clothes for you, then. Some oilskins that belong to my sister Fiona—if you don't mind borrowed clothes.'

'Not at all.'

'They're clean, I hasten to add, and you needn't fear that they're veterans of a dozen smelly fishing trips, because Fiona hates fishing. Put them on in the car.'

A few minutes later they were walking down to the car park together—although 'together' wasn't really how it would have looked to an outsider. Rourke was at least two metres from Prunella's side, as if fearful of an accidental touch. She was just as happy to keep her distance, of course.

'How is Lewis Moody?' she asked, mainly to fill the silence between them. Rourke had been providing Theatre staff with progress reports all week, as he made a twice-daily visit to the man from Harbour Deep during rounds.

'Still every indication that the leg is viable, and if Mr Moody had his way he'd already be at work on intensive physiotherapy.'

'I hate to think about the accident itself,' Prunella shuddered. 'Has he told you how on earth it came to happen?'

'No, he hasn't, but I can guess. A lot of people run these makeshift sawmilling set-ups to provide winter fuel. It's necessary, unfortunately, but it's really not safe. This isn't the first such accident Curtis Hospital has had to deal with over the years.'

'Not everyone uses wood fuel, though.'

'No, these days, with better transport, a lot of people use oil. In the old days, of course, it couldn't be brought in reliably. . .But is this really the sort of thing you want to talk about?'

'It's interesting,' she protested feebly.

They had reached the vehicle and he looked at her across its olive-green bonnet. 'You don't seem very relaxed.'

'Neither do you,' she retorted.

He laughed, showing very white but slightly crooked teeth. 'Perhaps you're right. It's not exactly clear what footing we're on with each other, is it?'

'What do you mean?'

'Well, I'll lay my cards on the table,' he said very firmly. 'I'm looking for friendship—nothing more. And I thought you'd like to see some whales, if we can.'

'That suits me fine,' she forced herself to say. 'Whales *and* friendship.'

'Good.'

They were still looking at each other across the car and for a long moment time seemed to be frozen, or perhaps it was just themselves. His face was very serious, his cheeks and jawline carved into angular planes, and his eyes like the sea, restlessly alive. A chill, capricious wind pulled at his dark hair, exposing the well-shaped ears that lay flat against his head. His mouth was closed and made a firm, steady shape of darker brown-pink against skin that had tanned considerably over the brief summer.

His gaze as usual was direct and somehow inspired confidence. Unfortunately in Prunella it always aroused much more disturbing feelings as well. Why did his eyes have to so closely match the colour of that turbulent, teeming Atlantic Ocean? Friendship wasn't what she wanted from him at all, but at least he was honest about it, so she had no cause to feel anger. A pity, as anger was sometimes an easier emotion than hurt and longing.

'Did I forget to unlock your side?' he queried gently at last, although he was standing there motionless with his hand on the door-handle just as she was.

'No, it's fine,' she mumbled, and opened the door, sliding on to the cool upholstery in her practical jeans.

'The dinghy is round near my mother's,' he said. 'It's not far.'

He took the road he had taken that first day with

Drifter, but they did not stop in to visit Mrs Donovan. The old woman, still stout and healthy in spite of her bent shape and harsh life, knew Prunella quite well by this time as a friend of Kathleen's. What she would make of this new 'friendship' between Prunella and Rourke, however, was another matter.

She was a quiet woman, always made a little shy by contact with people who had led far more wide-ranging lives than she had. Like her two eldest children, she could neither read nor write, and her pride in Rourke was tempered by embarrassment about her own ignorance, although she was in no way to blame for her lack of schooling. She was intelligent, too, with a perception that went beyond the kind of things learnt in a classroom.

I wouldn't fool her for a minute, Prunella thought to herself. If she saw me with Rourke, without a crowd of family and friends around, she'd know that friendship isn't what I really want.

So she was quite relieved when they continued past the old house and stopped where the road ended by the water. A number of small craft were moored there, and Prunella was trying to work out which one Rourke's might be when he said, 'See if you can guess,' gesturing at the boats so that his meaning was clear.

'The one with the red hull?'

He laughed. 'Way off, and I'm afraid you're going to be disappointed. It's this little blue dinghy here.'

'Oh.'

'I should have warned you.'

'Not at all. It'll be an adventure.'

'That's the spirit!'

'I won't ask you how much experience you've had with these contraptions, though, just in case it's something I don't want to know.'

He threw back his head and laughed, and warmth

filled her. It felt good to make him laugh, and that was something friends could do, wasn't it? Make each other laugh?

'I've had plenty of experience. And here's the waterproof gear.' He tossed the folded oilskins towards her, then shut the rear door of the vehicle.

'Is there anything else to bring?' she asked.

'No. There's fresh water in the boat in case of an emergency, or simply if we're thirsty. If something goes really wrong there are life-jackets and a couple of distress flares. But I didn't bother with food. We should be back by noon.'

'Uh-huh,' she nodded brightly. Mustn't let him guess that she had been looking forward to a whole day, and a delicious lazy picnic like that other Saturday three months ago. This was partly why she had guessed wrongly about the boat. It was a cold, gusty day with grey cloud in textured patches overhead, and the red-hulled boat had a cosy-looking cabin. She had imagined them cocooned there, perhaps even heating soup on a tiny cabin stove.

'If it looks too cold and bleak for you. . .' He had noticed her disappointment, but had misinterpreted it, fortunately.

'Not at all. As long as I'm warmly dressed, I love it like this. It's weather with character.'

'Spoken like an old campaigner. Good! I like a bit of bluster myself, and there's nothing dangerous forecast in the way of weather until tomorrow afternoon. Let's get going.'

He hauled the dinghy on to a tiny patch of rough shingle and helped her into it, seating her in the front so that he could sit within reach of the outboard motor and the attached rudder, which steered the boat by angling the motor itself. Prunella felt the wind freshen as soon as the boat left the shore, and quickly she put on the thick cream wool hat, scarf and gloves she had brought with her. Rourke's hands were gloved now too, and the hood of his oilskin shadowed his face so that she could see nothing above the bridge of that craggy nose.

She should have known that he would handle the boat expertly. Within a few minutes she had lost any sense of apprehension about the small craft and was facing into the wind, drinking in the exhilarating flavour of the salt-tanged air. They skimmed across the sheltered harbour, then came into the more open water that was French Bay. At once the sea became choppier, but Rourke steered the dinghy in a zigzag path that had them travelling with the flow of the waves.

They hugged the shoreline quite closely as they travelled south, and after a couple of miles Rourke shouted forward to Prunella, 'There were whales sighted off here a couple of days ago, apparently, so keep your eyes peeled from now on.'

But Prunella wasn't looking out to sea at all. She had caught sight of a low cottage of grey stone tucked into the hollow of a cove between two protective headlands. Its windows faced the sea, and even from this distance she could see cheerful curtains and bright kitchen blinds in warm tones that contrasted with the more sombre hues of the landscape. A two-tiered stone terrace was halfway to completion as well, and some hardy conifers were planted in rows along one side of the house at a distance of about twenty metres to give shelter, once they were grown, from the prevailing winds. It took her a full minute to realise what she was looking at.

'Rourke! That's your house!'

'Yes.' He seemed unmoved. 'Had you not realised we would be seeing it? It looks good from the water, doesn't it?'

'Yes. A perfect haven of a place in this landscape, and those windows are like welcoming eyes in a cool face.'

'Are they really?' he laughed.

'Did. . .did Meg help you choose the curtains?' she went on quickly, wondering if she had sounded too enthusiastic.

He frowned. 'No, I chose everything myself.'

It was a dampening response, and she wondered why. Surely Meg was no secret, when Kathleen seemed to be expecting an engagement announcement any day.

They were almost past the house now, however, and Prunella remembered that she was supposed to be looking out to sea. She turned away from the shore and began to watch the water, quickly mesmerised by the shifting patterns of white-cap and swell. Rourke slowed the motor until they were only just making way, and they chugged in wide circles, keeping close to the lee of the jutting cape to the south of them. About fifteen minutes went by, and nothing happened.

'Is this what fishing is like?' Prunella said.

'Yes—is it boring?'

'No! How could it be, when the sea is so alive, and the sky. . .? I don't think I've ever noticed the sky before.'

'Actually, it's looking a little more forbidding than the weather report led me to expect.'

'Should we go back?'

'Not yet. I'll keep an eye on it.'

They were silent for ten minutes more, then Rourke said suddenly, 'There!'

'What?' Prunella roused herself from her hypnotic focus on the sea. She had seen nothing move.

'Starboard side. At two o'clock, if this boat were the centre of a watch-face. It's gone now, a tail fin. That means a humpback, because the other three kinds you see around here don't show their tails while swimming. . . There it is again!'

'Yes! I saw it, the flick of a tail fin.'

'And there's its back. . .No! That looked like a minke.

If I'm right we're really lucky—two different types in one spot.'

'A minke? That's what I was hoping to see!' Prunella exclaimed, thinking of Kathleen's book.

'Really? They're the smallest.'

'I know, but there's something. . .' She didn't want to give away Katie's good news, knowing that the up-and-coming children's author would want to tell her favourite brother herself.

'Yes! Again!' Rourke said, unaware of this undercurrent. 'It's spouting. Look! And it *is* a minke. There's that small dorsal fin angled sharply backwards.'

'I wonder where the humpback has got to?'

'Perhaps it wasn't one after all. Just the minke and a trick of the light.'

'No,' Prunella said. 'Look! Out there. I couldn't see a tail fin, but that big back with that funny bumpy-shaped dorsal fin. . .'

'Yes, you're right. But it's moved quite a distance from us already. I doubt we'll see it again.'

The minke stayed well within sight range for several minutes longer, though, its sleek black back rising and falling again in an unpredictable place each time amid boiling white foam and rippling swell. It seemed to be keeping pace with their circling, as if taking a good look at these other creatures in its watery habitat, then finally it moved south, and their last sight of its curved shape was so brief that it wasn't worth waiting for.

'That was fabulous!' Prunella said, thinking that it seemed like a very good omen for Kathleen as well, and looking forward to telling her about it.

'You thought so?' Rourke said. 'I'm glad, because I think we're going to have to go back.' His voice was swept away by the wind so that she had to guess at the last words.

'Yes, it is getting choppier, isn't it?'

'And we're not equipped for anything resembling a storm.'

He turned the boat to the north and put the engine on full throttle. Prunella sat back to enjoy the trip. There was the stone cottage close by on the port side now. She turned to look at it and felt the wind catch at her scarf. In a second it had flown into the air, and without thinking she jumped to her feet to try and snatch it back.

'For goodness' sake——!' Rourke began.

It was all she heard. The dark water was an icy violation of every nerve in her body, and her head ached as if imprisoned in a vice when the freezing salty liquid closed over her. There had barely been time to realise that she was losing her balance, just the sensation of the bottom of the boat bucketing giddily beneath her feet and then, a second later, this.

Gasping, she fought to the surface and found the blessed air, gulping it in even as another smack of water hit her in the face so that half the breath was of choking, bitter water. The oilskins dragged at her body, which felt nearly numb already. The dinghy was nowhere to be seen, nor the shore, and the only sound was that of the sea in her ears and her own panic-stricken cries.

Then at last, after what seemed like minutes but was only as many seconds, came Rourke's voice, a fierce shout, 'Float! Lie back, tread water and *float*, Prunella! Don't *fight* it! *Float*! I can't get to you yet. I have to circle the dinghy, then cut the motor. I'm coming. I'm coming for you. Just tread water and *float*!'

Of everything he said, only two things made sense— that he was coming for her and that she had to float. Float. Tread water and float. With an enormous effort of will she tried to slow her breathing, ignore the cold and the dragging at her limbs, and tilt her head and torso back so that by gently moving arms and legs she could stay above water. She still could not see Rourke, and desperately wanted to turn and look for him, but knew that she had to resist this desire. The more frenetically she moved, the more she would tire and the more likely she would be to swallow dangerous quantities of sea water.

If only he would come! The cold of the water pressed on her like some medieval torture device and she felt fear, too, about the depths below her. Whales were friendly enough, but what other creatures lurked beneath her pale, fragile body?

At last he was there. The blue side of the dinghy bobbed beside her, like a cliff, it seemed—far too high for her to climb aboard. But his strong hands gripped her beneath each arm. 'Kick as hard as you can, Prunella.'

She did so, not understanding at first, then she felt her body rise in the water, propelled by the motion of her feet at the same time as she was pulled from above. The boat rocked dangerously, then steadied as she lay, sprawled and gasping, along the wooden bench seat. At first she was too concerned simply with breathing freely to think about what Rourke was doing, then she felt him coax her off the seat.

'Lie down in the bottom of the boat. Quick!'

She did so, cramped and uncomfortable against the rough wood with its layer of sand and salt. What was he doing? A heavy, stiff sheet of canvas tarpaulin came down on top of her and she felt as if she were a piece of cargo, a crate of fish. Then she heard the dinghy's engine roar into life, and her frozen cheek thumped painfully against the boat's hull as they smacked down into a trough between two waves. Only shock and cold kept her from crying at the awfulness of it, and she was too stunned to realise that what Rourke was doing was for her own good.

In moments he had run the dinghy up on to the shore,

finding the only place where a boat could land without damaging its hull. There was a splash as he jumped into the shallow water, then he pulled the canvas from her and lifted her out of the boat.

'Can you walk? Run?'

'Of course I——No! My legs!'

'Too cold.' Without another word he had wrapped the stiff, rough canvas around her again and was carrying her up to the little stone house.

Inside, she barely registered furniture, carpets and prints on the walls. Rourke began to peel away oilskins, hat and gloves, all of which were sodden and dripping. She had begun to shake violently now and he knew without her having to say anything that her own numb fingers were useless.

When her outer clothing was off he carried her to the bedroom, where a bed stood already made up with thick continental quilt and fat new pillows. She made no protest as he continued to undress her, by now dimly aware that she was dangerously cold and he was carrying out the required treatment for hypothermia—remove all clothing, cover the patient with thick bedding and cradle her in your own body warmth.

She was only naked in front of him for a moment. He sat her on the edge of the bed as he gently removed two lacy powder-blue wisps of underwear, then deftly rolled back the quilt and slid her between the sheets. She was still shaking and felt no warmth yet at all. If he gave a shuddering gasp as he slipped her into the bed it could have been simply that he was cold himself after holding her dripping body against him in that wind.

She closed her eyes and lay on her side, visited now by nightmare flashbacks to those awful minutes in the water, flashbacks that would not leave her for some days to come. Her shaking increased, and when she felt him cradle her shape from behind, dressed only in dry cotton

underwear, she did not think of the fact that it was
Rourke, only that it was warmth, safety and comfort.

'You're safe now, love,' he said, and she felt his warm
breath whispering gently against her neck. 'You're fine
now—warm, dry, cosy. You'll stop shivering soon.'

With hands still stiff from cold she gripped the arm
that had come around her, and felt its soft hair and
firmly sculptured muscles. When his hands began to
caress the life and circulation back into her skin, moulding hips, thighs and soft flat belly, she at first thought
only of how soothing it felt and how blessedly warm,
then at the same time as a more female awareness came
to her she dipped into a deep, relaxing cloud of sleep. . .

Rourke was gone when she woke, and it could have
been two hours later or only twenty minutes. She
stretched like a cat, feeling the sheets warm against the
nakedness of her skin. On the pillow her hair was dry. It
must have been a long sleep, then. Sitting up and holding
the quilt against her breasts, she saw that the door of the
room was ajar. The air felt warm, and an image came
back to her of a fire laid ready to light in the grate of the
newly furnished house. Rourke must have put a match
to it to heat the place up.

On the edge of the bed she saw a silk dressing-gown,
very masculine in maroon and navy with wide lapels
and a twisted tasselled cord. She guessed it was for her
own use and slipped it on, feeling too naked beneath it
still, but knowing that her own clothes would not yet be
dry.

There were no slippers, and when she padded down
the corridor silently in her bare feet and entered the
lounge she realised that Rourke didn't know she was
awake yet. He sat by the fire, and stared broodingly into
it. He wore jeans, but his torso was still bare and his
skin glowed warmly in the light of the orange flames,

while the rest of the room had the dimness of late
afternoon.

'It must be late,' she blurted unthinkingly as she
approached him, and he turned on a hiss of breath.

'You're awake!'

'Yes. I've been asleep for too long.'

'It's about four. Your body needed the sleep. I wasn't
going to wake you.'

'It seems later than that.'

'Look at the weather. That's why it seems dark.'

Through the half-open cream and navy curtains she
saw that the clouds had lowered and darkened, and were
spattering raindrops against the window-panes like
handfuls of gravel roughly thrown. The wind was much
stronger now too.

'Come and sit by the fire,' he suggested, reaching out
for his flannel shirt as he spoke and pulling his arms
through its sleeves quickly.

'I should get dressed. Do you have anything that
would fit me—or are my things dry?' she added, noticing
that he had them hanging over the brand-new brass and
iron fire-screen.

'Only these,' he answered, taking her underwear and
tossing it to her.

She was embarrassed at the scantiness of the gar-
ments, and balled them in her hand before shoving them
into the pocket of the dressing-gown. She wasn't going
to put them on until she had something else to put on
top!

'We should be getting back to town, shouldn't we?'
she persisted when the blue lace was safely hidden away.

He raised one black eyebrow, his green eyes glinted
and his lips curved in a half-smile. 'And how do you
suggest we do that?'

'The——Oh!' His Land Rover was parked by the
harbour in St Anthony, and the dinghy. . .Leaving aside

the fact that it was the last place she wanted to be after this morning's dangerous dunking, she could tell without asking that he wouldn't risk putting to sea in this weather.

But he made it explicit anyway. 'We'd have been fine if we'd got back at noon, as planned. But there's no way I'm risking the trip by boat now.'

'Then. . .?'

'The phone's not connected yet. I suggest we stay the night and walk back to town first thing tomorrow morning. There isn't a great deal to eat, I'm afraid. Tinned soup—which is already hot—crackers, cheese, tea. No milk or sugar.'

'Food? I'm not thinking of that!' she exclaimed frankly. 'It's——'

'Don't worry, you'll get the bed,' he interrupted gently, anticipating her comment.

'Oh! Yes, well, I couldn't help noticing that the spare room is filled with cardboard boxes and nothing else.'

'I borrowed Devlin's truck last night and did the move,' Rourke answered. 'I got pretty involved in it and stayed up all night getting things straight, but I haven't got all the furniture I need yet—and that includes a spare bed—and I didn't get all the boxes unpacked.'

'I wasn't criticising the accommodation,' she said hastily. 'It all looks lovely.' In fact, the crimson-toned Persian carpet was just as she had imagined more than three months ago when furnishing the unfinished house in her mind, and the low, velour-upholstered couch in a subtle stripe of steel and French grey looked very inviting.

'Then sit down and get comfortable,' Rourke said. He gestured to the empty space beside him on the couch, then reached towards the fire and took a saucepan off a makeshift wire grill he had set up there. 'It might be a long evening. I haven't got the generator running yet, so there's no electricity, and I only have two candles.' He grinned as he poured steaming vegetable soup into a thick cream china mug for her. 'It's shaping up like some scene from a horror film, isn't it?'

Or like a classic seduction, Prunella added to herself. The problem was, he had no desire to seduce her, while her own senses were frighteningly willing, even though her mind said in a panicky way, Don't let him get close. Don't touch him again at all.

She sipped the thick soup in silence for several minutes while Rourke poked at the fire, adding more wood and exposing the hottest coals so that they blazed up with sparks and crackles, flooding the dim room with glowing light and warmth.

'At least my clothes will be dry by tomorrow,' she said, feeling the heat on the V of skin below her neck that was exposed by the crossed front of the silk dressing-gown.

'Meanwhile, that thing looks a lot better on you than it does on me,' he said, a silky caress in his tone. 'I'm certainly in no hurry for you to change.'

'Don't,' she said, putting down the now empty mug and wrapping the gown more closely around her. 'We've agreed that we're. . .friends. Let's not spoil it with meaningless flirting.'

'Who says this is flirting?'

She looked at him steadily, her heart thumping, and when he slid towards her on the couch her arms reached out for him of their own accord. As soon as they touched, memory came flooding back to her of the way he had felt when they had lain together in the bed, and she longed to be there with him again, this time not cradled gently by his curved shape but tangled together in a fever of limbs and torsos.

Here on the couch, though, he was slow, caressing her jaw first with his smooth hand before bringing her face to his and finding her lips in a long sweet kiss that sent tendrils of fire all through her. After a long time in which nothing existed for her but his mouth she felt him slip his warm hand into the crossed folds of the gown until he found her bare waist, and she knew that the silky material was gradually parting to reveal her completely to him.

'Friends?' He breathed the mocking question hoarsely. 'Oh, lord, Prunella Murdoch, I don't know what I want any more, but friendship can be the most insipid word in the world at times like this!'

He pulled her even more closely to him and she felt the softness of his flannel shirt and the firmer fabric of his jeans against her bare flesh. When his fingers found the tasselled cord around her waist and undid its bow she made no protest, and wanted to search for his skin in the same way. If the rest of him felt and smelled anything like this warm column of neck and these living waves of hair. . .

CHAPTER EIGHT

THE pounding at the door startled both of them into breaking instantly apart.

'Rourke? Are you there? Rourke!' came a male voice.

'Coming!' The word came out as a hoarse bark. 'Wait, can you?'

But it was too late. Few people locked their front doors in St Anthony, and Rourke was no exception. Before he had even finished speaking Prunella heard the noise of the wind rise as the door was opened. Breathless and overwhelmed, she hugged the robe quickly around her, but had no time to tie the cord, and suspected anyway that her fingers would only fumble uselessly with the slippery silk.

She huddled down into the couch and wished she needed not turn round to greet the intruder. There was a separate entrance hall to this cottage, as there was in most Newfoundland houses. It was necessary in order to keep out the worst of the weather, and heavy footsteps were now through the second door and into the room where they sat.

Rourke was on his feet by this time. 'Oh, it's you, Dev. Come in,' he added unnecessarily, the gruff tone sounding forced to Prunella's sensitive ears.

'Was out myself today in *Lady Pat*. Just got back when the weather came down and saw you weren't in yet. Didn't want Mum to worry. Came to check here first. What happened?'

Prunella had turned around and pulled herself higher in the couch during his laconic explanation, and he greeted her with a quick nod. Like his mother, he knew

her as Kathleen's friend, but if he felt any surprise at
finding her here alone with Rourke he didn't show it.
She knew, though, that her cheeks were on fire and had
to fight the temptation to lift a hand to her hair in a
futile attempt to smooth out the tangles Rourke's fingers
had made.

'Prunella fell overboard,' Rourke said, adding gener-
ously and untruthfully, 'not her fault. The wind caught
her scarf and she lost her balance. Luckily we were just
offshsore here, so we came straight in. Her clothes still
aren't dry, as you can see.' He gestured at the silk
dressing-gown. 'And by the time she was warm the
weather had closed in.'

'Couldn't you have walked back in?'

Rourke put a hand to his hair and rumpled it,
laughing awkwardly as he did so. 'I didn't think it was
that urgent, Dev. I hadn't told Mum we were going out
in the boat, and she can't see where it's moored from her
windows. I was going to walk cross-country to Conche
Cove later on and use someone's phone there to call the
hospital and you, since you knew I was out today.'

'I've wasted a trip, then,' Devlin said, looking from
Rourke to Prunella and back again. 'Sorry. I'll get out
of your way.'

'No, you certainly haven't wasted a trip,' Prunella put
in firmly, standing as she did so and praying that she
didn't look as underdressed in this gown as she felt.
'We'd both be very glad of a lift back to town. We'd
given up hope. Rourke, if you could find those clothes
you were going to lend me I can put them on and we
can get going.'

'Of course,' he nodded evenly, already striding from
the room. Prunella saw that relief blazed in his face.
What had he been afraid of? That she was going to
happily say goodbye to Devlin, then suggest they pick

up where they left off? Rourke added, 'I'll only be a moment.'

In fact, he was about ten minutes. Prunella could hear the sound of cartons being moved and opened, and guessed that he hadn't yet unpacked all his clothes. Meanwhile Devlin went to the fire and reached his hands out to warm them, turning his back to Prunella as if awkward and uncertain about her presence.

He only spoke once. 'Didn't think the weather would turn like this.'

'No, Rourke was surprised, too,' Prunella murmured in reply.

When Rourke emerged he was carrying grey tracksuit trousers, a red and black tartan flannel shirt, and a black wool pullover. 'You've got your underwear in your pocket, there, haven't you?' he said.

'Yes.' Again she was embarrassed. The pockets of the dressing-gown weren't big enough to hold much in the way of underclothing, and Devlin Donovan now knew more about what she had been wearing today than she was happy with. Rourke did too, for that matter.

'You'll have to put up with damp socks and shoes, though,' he said.

'Only till I get home,' she answered, heading for the blue and white tiled bathroom.

Just as she had finished dressing there was a knock at the door and Rourke was standing there, holding her almost dry socks and wetter leather running shoes.

'Ready for these?' he said.

'Yes.' She folded her arms protectively in front of her after she had taken the shoes and socks. She swam in his clothes. The waistband of the trousers was rolled three times, and the sleeves of shirt and pullover were pushed up into bunches at each elbow. She couldn't help thinking of the first time she had worn something of his, on the day they had met. If they hadn't rescued Drifter together that day, would things be different now?

'Good,' Rourke said, as she took the shoes and socks. Then he added in a lower tone, 'And I think we'd both agree that Dev's arrival was a blessing in disguise, wouldn't we?'

'Definitely,' she answered.

'Good,' he said again. 'Let's hope this means we can stay out of trouble in future.'

'Yes.'

'And perhaps. . .stay out of each other's way altogether?' he added on a slightly questioning note.

She forced herself to nod coolly, but could not meet his eyes. Instead she focused on the column of his throat, just where it disappeared smoothly into the open neck of his dark blue shirt.

'Friendship was a good idea in theory,' she said matter-of-factly. 'In practice it doesn't seem to have worked out. That's clear to both of us, isn't it?'

'Very,' he nodded. 'What civilised creatures we both are!'

'Indeed.' Her head gave a crisp little jerk of assent and her white teeth were held tightly together.

'Put those shoes on, then, and we'll see you out the front. I'm going to screen off the fire and get a bag for your clothes.'

Half an hour later she was alone in her room and the ghastly episode was over. Had she succeeded in convincing Devlin that her state of undress was purely the result of her icy dunking? Perhaps it didn't matter. As Rourke had suggested, his arrival was actually the best thing that had happened all day.

But later that night in bed, as the wind whistled around the residence building, she couldn't help thinking about the stone house. Rourke had gone straight back there after collecting his Land Rover and a few more provisions. Now he was probably wrapped in the feathery quilt on that big new bed, and in spite of everything her treacherous body still wanted him, wanted to go back to the time today when they had lain in that bed together. Her powerful desire overshadowed even the nightmare flashbacks to her time in the freezing water.

If I can't get him out of my system, she thought miserably, what on earth am I going to do?

The last patient on Dr Donovan's list had just been wheeled away to Recovery when the call came. They were already running late today, after an exploratory laparotomy had revealed cancer of the colon in a fifty-three-year-old woman.

'There's an emergency appendectomy coming in', Barbara McKay reported. 'Rourke, I think it's a niece of yours, Julia Donovan.'

Prunella looked across at him. The nursing team was taking a brief break while the theatre was being cleaned. Due in next was Alan Kerson to operate on a cruciate ligament injury, but he and the patient would have to wait even longer now. Rourke had been on the point of leaving to do some paperwork, having gulped a quick coffee as he unwound from the strain of such concentrated work. Now he had to summon his energy again. She saw that it was an effort for him. He had been up all the previous night, apparently, dealing with three patients injured in a steam-pipe explosion aboard a fishing trawler.

And now he had to operate on little Julia Donovan. It was three weeks now since that day when Kathleen had first shown Prunella her whale story. Julia had been home from school with a stomach upset then, and had apparently complained of pain and nausea since then as well.

I wonder if I should have picked it up? Prunella thought.

But, apart from the time when she had been at Conlan and Daphne's, she had only heard second-hand about the child's recurring ailment, and Kathleen had said, 'Daphne suspects she's just making it up. She's not taking too well to school so far.' As usual, however, Prunella felt her professional responsibility on an emotional level even when reason told her that she was not to blame.

How did Rourke feel, though? This was the daughter of the brother he felt so bitter about. Did his feelings extend to the younger generation as well? She saw that he was frowning, and that he still held the white coffee-cup, although it was empty. He was fiddling with it in a restless way that was unlike him. . .

Surely he couldn't let the thing with Conlan influence him during surgery? she thought to herself, horrified. Was she imagining deliberate carelessness? No, but it was the kind of situation where complicated feelings could cause distraction, which led to unthinking mistakes. It's probably unnecessary, but I'm going to watch this operation extra carefully, she decided.

Over the past three weeks she and Rourke had kept to their avowed intention of steering well clear of one another. She didn't know what it had done for him, but it hadn't helped her at all. Kathleen still speculated to her frequently about the situation with Meg, and Rourke's physical presence in and around Theatre Two still made her pulses race.

I can't talk about distracting influences! she realised miserably.

Twenty minutes later Julia was wheeled in, already drowsy from pre-medication. She recognised neither her Uncle Rourke, nor Prunella, which was hardly surprising, since they must appear to be very alien forms in their scrub suits, gowns, caps and masks.

'May we start, Dr Hughes?' Rourke always went through the formality of asking his anaesthetists this question, although many surgeons were not so courteous.

'Yes, she's looking good,' the anaesthetist replied.

'Dr Green, would you like to handle this?' Rourke said straight away. 'And, Mr Scioto, I'd like your comments on what she's doing.'

'Fine,' the medical student nodded, and Karen Green draped the small patient and prepared to make the first incision straight away.

Rourke observed closely but participated only minimally, and Prunella, very involved herself in passing instruments and holding clamps, wondered if he was standing back deliberately because this was his brother Conlan's child.

No, I'm reading too much into it, she decided. After all, it was part of his job to give Karen Green the right sort of experience.

'So, Mr Scioto, does this need to come out, or can we leave it?' Rourke said when they got to the offending appendix.

'It needs to come out. No doubt at all.'

The appendix was swollen and inflamed, and Prunella could easily have given as confident a response as Joe Scioto's.

'Lucky we got to it today, in fact, wouldn't you say?' Rourke suggested, and again the medical student agreed. He had relaxed a lot lately, but was still a bundle of annoying mannerisms that would probably drive his team mad years from now when he was a top-notch surgeon in his own right.

Dr Green closed up the patient, the equipment count was found to be correct and Dr Hughes adjusted the medication to bring her close to the surface of consciousness. She would come to full awareness in the recovery-room, where Prunella guessed that her parents would be waiting.

Meanwhile her own shift was coming to an end, since it was nearly three o'clock. She could hand over to Maureen O'Shaunessy, who would scrub for Alan Kerson's operation and anything else that came up that afternoon. In the change area and wash-room, Prunella took off her scrubs and put on day clothes—teal-blue wool trousers and a cream blouse topped by a black cardigan jacket—then added a touch of make-up.

Some people rushed off home straight away after surgery, but she liked to use this time to wind down a little, to stretch out face muscles that had stiffened into lines of concentration, and to start planning the rest of her day. Today she was intending to shop at Viking Mall, and as she walked through the rotunda she mentally created a list of the things she needed to buy.

Then, out of the corner of her eye, she saw a figure rise from one of the comfortable chairs and aim itself in her direction. Turning, she found that it was Conlan Donovan.

'Hello, Prue,' he said awkwardly. 'I saw you and. . .' He stopped.

'Hello, Conlan.' She greeted him in a friendly way with a light touch on his forearm. 'You can go into Recovery, you know, and be with Julia when she wakes up.'

'Oh, you know about it?' He looked relieved at not having to explain why he was here.

'I was the scrub nurse during the operation.'

'Yes, Daphne's with her now in Recovery,' he said, going back to her earlier words. 'But I like it better out here. I'll see Julia when she goes upstairs, later on, like.'

'There's nothing to worry about, Conlan. She's going to be fine.'

'I know, but I'm not that keen on hospitals.'

'Aren't you?' Was this a clue to his feelings about Rourke?

'This is my favourite part of the whole place.' He gave a sweeping gesture that took in the whole of the Jordi Bonet mural. 'I don't know why I like that thing. . .art and such-like. . .but I do.'

'I do too.'

'Well, you'll be wanting to get off home. . .'

'You really mustn't worry, Con,' she said to him again. His blue eyes looked tired and dispirited in that heavy, seagoing face. Then she added without thinking, 'Rourke and the team did an excellent job as usual, and——'

'*Rourke* did it?' Tiredness vanished and was replaced instantly by bristling anger.

'Y-yes,' she stammered, cursing her thoughtlessness. 'General surgery—it's his field. I thought you'd know——'

'Why would I know? How would I know anything? He's some great doctor, and I can barely recognise the letters in my own name. I was already in the fishery when he was born, and when we got told he was bright I had to give part of my wages each week so he could stay at school. He should have stayed on the mainland. He shouldn't have come back pretending he could repay us. Repay us? There's nothing can repay the way his life's different from mine. I swore I'd never take any help from him, and now he's tricked me. He's done that appendix on Julia, and Daphne's going to be nagging at me again, "Why can't we take some help from Rourke? You'd take it from the others, from Finlay. Finlay had the same chances as Rourke and you don't hate him." Of course I don't hate him! He failed, and doesn't that make me a mean-spirited man? To forgive one man's failure and hate another's success!'

He pounded one fist into the palm of the other hand in a gesture of impotent anger and shame, and Prunella, who had listened helplessly to his tirade of confession, had not the slightest idea what to do. He had been speaking in a low, emotion-filled tone, and the foyer was empty at the moment, although soon people would begin to gather in wait for afternoon visiting hour to begin. Still, whoever was on the switchboard must be aware that something was going on. Prunella risked a nervous glance across to the desk. It was Beth Stewart today, unfortunately, not Alison Harriman, who might have known how to help her brother.

He was continuing, trembling as he spoke. 'I'm going to leave St Anthony. Daphne says we can't afford to leave, but if Rourke stays I'm going to leave. It's got too much for me here.'

Prunella could see that these tumbling words, anger-filled though they were, were only the tip of the iceberg, and that years of bitter, unexpressed feeling boiled away inside the man. When the door opened and Rourke entered the rotunda, papers fluttering in his hand and an abstracted frown on his face, there was a quality of inevitability that made each moment stand out very clearly.

Rourke hadn't seen Conlan, but Conlan saw Rourke. He broke off his emotional diatribe and strode towards his younger brother, his stocky body moving awkwardly. Prunella had not realised until now, seeing them together for the first time, how much taller and better-formed Rourke was. The surgeon looked up in time to ward off the tighly balled fist aimed at his jaw, but not in time to protect his papers, which fanned on to the polished floor in a hissing rustle.

The men were locked together now, evenly matched in spite of the many disparities between them. Rourke had height, youth and health, but Conlan had the strength of someone who had worked hard physically all his life, and he had anger as well. He grunted as he grappled with his brother and his face reddened ominously. Their feet scuffled over the strewn papers, tearing and marking them, and Prunella did not dare to try and gather them up lest she become caught in the mêlée herself.

Then she heard Rourke's voice speaking desperately in a tone she had never heard him use before. 'Con, Con, don't do this. What can I do? I've tried every way I know to pay back——' He broke off, no energy left to waste on speech.

Prunella saw now that he wasn't returning his brother's blows, but was simply trying to contain them and ward them off, and inevitably this meant that he was getting the worst of the fight. It had travelled several feet across the room now, and Rourke had to struggle to stay on his feet. Conlan was trying to get him down.

But at least Prunella could get to the papers now. Darting forward, she slid them into one heap, then found the manila folder that had held them. It was the draft of a research paper, she saw—something about the incidence of diverticulitis in the Inuit population of northern Labrador. There was no time to take in anything more, however. Conlan had succeeded in bringing Rourke to the floor and now it was a tussle for supremacy. Whoever ended on top. . .

Heavy footsteps sounded on the floor. Security had arrived, paged by Beth Stewart the moment the fight had begun. The two uniformed men assessed the situation at a glance and in tandem pulled Conlan away and held him firmly by both upper arms. Rourke sprang to his feet, his face white and tightly controlled. Breath snorted through his tensed nostrils. He would have been panting if he had opened his mouth. Then Prunella saw why he held his lips so firmly closed. There was blood there, escaping at one corner, and she guessed that his mouth was full of it.

'You're hurt, Rourke,' she whispered.

He shook his head.

'Yes, you are,' she insisted. 'Here.'

There was a handkerchief in her pocket and she pressed it into his hand. He brought it to his face straight away and when he spat into it a bloodstain spread in seconds. As soon as he had wiped his lips enough to speak, he did so. 'Let him go, Murray,' he said to the head security man, then forestalled the man's reply. 'No, don't go to the police. I'm not going to bring charges. Let him go.'

'I'm not sure that we can, Dr Donovan,' Murray Tilson said slowly. 'The hospital's involved, not just yourself.'

'Please——' Rourke began again.

'For God's sake, Rourke,' Conlan muttered, 'let him call the police.'

He was sagging and defeated now, and even while she longed to treat the swelling that was already starting around Rourke's mouth, Prunella had to feel sorry for the older man. It seemed almost a relief to him to be led away to face charges relating to the disturbance he had created. One or two people had started to gather for visiting hours now, and they looked at him curiously, but very quickly the foyer had returned to its normal quiet state. Only Rourke, with his hand still pressing Prunella's inadequate handkerchief to his face, betrayed the fact that something had been going on.

'Got another handkerchief?' he said through his fingers.

'Yes. Here.' She found another one. Fortunately it was also clean. 'Give me the old one,' she said.

'Let me keep it and wash it.'

'Don't be silly!'

'Please,' he insisted. 'It's got half a tooth in it, among other things.'

'Oh.'

'Look, I need a bit of fixing up,' he said, his vowels and consonants sounding thicker than usual through his swelling lip. 'And I don't want to go to Casualty. I'm sure you can understand why.'

'Of course. Come to my apartment.'

'I hate to do this to you. . .'

'Not at all. It's an emergency.' She spoke as briskly as she could, but they were both aware of the undercurrent that ran between them. This was an event that broke through the distance they had each agreed to maintain. If she refused to help him, though, it would only call more attention to the fact that such an agreement was necessary. 'Come on,' she said. 'Let's not waste time.'

'My paper. . .'

'It's here. Pages out of order, probably, and some of them are marked and crumpled.'

'It's only a draft. Thanks for thinking of it.'

'Is it likely that I'd have left it spread out on the floor?'

She led the way out of the building and across the car park to the staff apartments, remembering thankfully that her room was especially neat and tidy at the moment after a thorough overhaul yesterday evening. She would be able to come up with all the necessary first-aid equipment straight away.

'You've got a new print,' he said after she had ushered him through the door. He was looking at a reproduction of a soft nineteenth-century English landscape.

'Yes, my friend Emma sent it from Scotland for my birthday.'

'Your birthday? When was that?'

'Two weeks ago.'

'And you didn't tell me.'

She didn't bother to reply, although she wanted to point out that they were no longer on a footing that made talking about birthdays together appropriate.

'I don't think you've mentioned Emma before, either.'

This time she retorted crisply, 'That's because I hadn't forgiven her for leaving me in the lurch over the job here.'

'How "in the lurch"?'

'She was supposed to come too—it was actually her idea—but she got married instead.'

'But you've forgiven her now?'

'Yes.'

'Which means you like it here.'

Again she didn't reply, being busy in the tiny *en suite* bathroom finding cotton wool, antiseptic, ointment and dressings. But he appeared in the doorway and found her gaze in the mirror. 'Prunella?'

She looked steadily at the glass, seeing his capable hand pressed against the door-jamb and his swelling mouth held in a firm line. 'Sorry, I didn't realise it was a question,' she said. 'Yes, I like it here now. I've decided to stay for a second year.' In fact it was a decision she only made as she spoke the words, and she would have bitten them back if she could. Why commit herself like that, just because she wanted to prove to Rourke that he was of no importance in her life, and because he must never have cause to think that her hopeless feeling for him had been strong enough to drive her away from St Anthony? 'If you could bring that desk chair over and sit here in the doorway,' she went on. 'This fluorescent mirror light is the strongest and clearest.'

'Sure,' he answered briefly, and had swung the chair into position seconds later.

She stood over him, angled so that her own shadow did not block the light, and began to sponge his face with balls of wet cotton wool, taking an inventory of his injuries as she did so. He sat with his eyes closed, his dark lashes forming two thick crescents against each cheek. His top lip was split and the gum had been torn by that broken bit of tooth. His left cheek was swollen and reddened, and would be blue and bruised-looking by tomorrow. There was a long scratch there too, and on the inside of the cheek she could see blood still welling.

'You really need a stitch or two in this cheek,' she said.

'Nonsense!' He spat her fingers out of his mouth.

'All right,' she nodded, 'I know you're reluctant to go to Casualty. I'll pad it with gauze and hope it closes up on its own. Hope you weren't planning any long phone conversations this evening.'

'Why phone, in particular?'

'Oh. . .' she had actually been thinking of Meg in Toronto '. . .just because the phone is less distinct anyway.'

'Well, I wasn't.'

'Sorry?'

'Wasn't planning any.'

'Good. I won't put antiseptic on the gauze because it's not likely to get infected inside your mouth.'

'I'm glad you think so highly of my oral hygiene.'

'Please, Rourke.'

He opened his eyes and looked at her, then grabbed her wrists with firm hands and brought them to her sides. 'Don't you think a joke or two might help us to relax?' he said gently.

'I'm perfectly relaxed,' she snapped back, hating the fact that his touch on her wrists made her want to reach for him and know again the feel of him in her arms.

'You don't seem very relaxed,' he returned mildly. 'Your arms are as rigid as sticks.'

'I'm tired.'

'All right, and so am I, since I was up all night. Believe me, I'm as anxious to finish—ow!——' he broke off and tried the word again more carefully '—*finish*. . .those fs hurt. . .as you are.'

'Good. Well, if you'll stop making jokes and criticising the way I respond to them. . .'

She didn't finish the sentence and he said nothing in reply, but dropped her arms and closed his eyes again. Carefully she wadded two gauze pads in between cheek and gum to protect the open cut on the inside of his mouth and sponged the cleaned breaks in his skin on cheek and lip with mild antiseptic. 'I don't need to tell you how to look after that bruise,' she said.

'Mm, I've got ice at home. But I haven't got deep-heat ointment, and my left shoulder feels as if it's going to stiffen up badly. Do you happen to——?'

'Yes, here it is.' She produced the tube. 'Have it. I don't need it back.'

'Thanks, but I'll need you to put it on. It's my lats. . .sorry, my latidimus dorsi——'

'Yes, I know what it is.'

'—and I can't reach it.' He began to pull his buttoned white shirt off over his head and then stopped, wincing. 'In fact, I'll need you to take off this shirt!'

He stood up and, setting her teeth, Prunella reached for the buttons. 'I'm going to do it the civilised way,' she said. 'Using the buttons for their intended purpose.'

'Whatever's easiest,' he answered, wincing again and taking in a sharp hiss of breath as she slid the shirt-sleeves down his arm.

'If it's that sore. . .'

'No. I'm not going to Physio. It can heal on its own.'

He turned and leaned his forehead against the wall while she squeezed the deep-heat ointment on to her fingers. His back was smooth and perfectly sculpted, each muscle and vertebra visible. She touched her hand to his shoulder and began to rub the white cream in, using firm circular motions. 'Does it hurt too much?' she asked.

'Only as it's supposed to, and. . .ahhh!. . .that deep heat really is hot. Keep going!'

She did so, until the cream had created a wide red circle on his supple flesh. 'It's all rubbed in now,' she said. 'Will that do?'

'For now. I might see if Katie is free to spend the night at the house and she can continue the treatment— if I can stay awake long enough for another course of it.'

'Yes, go and get some rest,' she agreed, easing the shirt back on. The cream gave off a pungent menthol smell that masked his musky male scent, but all her other senses were headily aware of him and she was tired of the effort of maintaining her control.

'Prunella. . .' He turned to her in the doorway.

'Yes?'

'I needn't ask you not to say anything about today's. . .drama to anyone.'

'No, you *needn't* ask. Obviously I wouldn't.'

'It'll be all over the hospital by now anyway, so I don't know why I'm making a point of it, and of course my family will know eventually too.'

'Rourke, isn't there some way it can be solved? Might not today have been a crisis that———?'

'No.' He shook his head curtly. 'It's been going on too long, and it runs too deep. I've tried everything I know. I help him financially, but he doesn't know it. He thinks it's money Mum saves from an insurance pay-out. And anything else I do for him is managed in the same way.'

'Drifter's rescue, for instance?'

'Yes. How did you know?'

'Something you said at the time. It just clicked into place.'

'Mum told him someone had found Drifter and brought him to her place.'

'You should be angry, Rourke, but you're not, are you? You're hurt. It really pains you. Why?'

'Isn't it obvious?' Words were an effort, clearly, with his injured face, but Prunella sensed that he wanted to speak. 'I can put myself in his place so clearly, and I know I'd be just as bitter. To feel that an accident of birth order made one brother the golden boy and the other a struggling nobody.'

'He's not a nobody. He's a beloved husband and father.'

'Yes, but he's also a man with abilities that can never be used.'

'How do you know? Devlin and Dermot——'

'Are happy,' he finished. 'They're men of average needs and ambitions. Conlan is considerably more intelligent than I am, more gifted in other ways, too, and nothing can ever, ever come of it now.' He spoke the words with heavy finality, then added quickly, 'See you in surgery tomorrow.'

He was gone before she could say anything more.

CHAPTER NINE

'FINLAY'S going to pick us up at about five,' Kathleen said, then added more loudly and in her most authoritative tone, 'Julia, you're supposed to be in bed.'

'I am,' came a small voice from the bedroom Julia shared with her three older sisters.

'OK, then why can I hear footsteps on the floor?'

'I just had to get up to fetch my doll. But now I'm in bed.'

'All right, then,' Kathleen said resignedly, rolling her eyes at Prunella as they sat in the kitchen at Conlan and Daphne's, drinking tea and eating cake.

The little girl had been discharged from hospital two days earlier and was still convalescent in the eyes of her doctors, if not her own. It was Friday afternoon, and there was a house-warming party at Rourke's tonight. Prunella, invited to the affair as a general friend of the family, had brought along her outfit at Kathleen's invitation, and they would change here at Conlan's before, as Kathleen had just explained, Finlay transported them and several others in his rather battered old car.

'What's the time now?' Prunella asked.

'Fourish. We'll finish our tea and then take turns in the shower, shall we?'

'Sounds good.' Prunella hoped Kathleen didn't realise how little she was looking forward to the evening.

She saw quite enough of Rourke during working hours without having to socialise with him as well. But it would look too much as though she was avoiding him if she didn't go. She could plead the fact that she was on call—but then Rourke was on call as well. At least with most of the Donovan clan present it would have to be a fairly large gathering. With any luck she would manage to get lost in the crowd and need not speak to Rourke at all once she had given him the small present she had purchased.

'You take the first shower,' Kathleen said when they had finished their tea and cake, and she refused to listen to Prunella's polite protests that she would be just as happy to go second.

Prunella took the towel and toiletries she had brought and went downstairs, where a garage, bath and laundry formed the lower level of the back half of the house. Since the place was built on sloping ground, the front half of the house had only a single storey. It was dim down here, and before entering the bathroom she took little notice of what the garage and laundry contained, muttering to herself, 'Where's the light?' after a painful bump on the hip from the corner of the washing-machine.

The bathroom was clean but crowded with towels and toothbrushes, so she changed her mind about putting on make-up in here and contented herself after her shower with slipping into the party dress that she hoped would be right for the evening. A black velvet bodice with a wide neck complemented a shot-silk skirt of midnight-blue and sea-green that was gathered very fully into the low waist. The puffed elbow-length sleeves were of the same silk, and though it was simply cut, without flounces or bows, it looked expensive and dressy, and she hadn't worn it once since she had arrived in St Anthony.

If Kathleen says it's too much I'll race home and get my purple jersey dress, she thought, gathering her things and coming out through the laundry and into the garage.

She had left the lights on for Kathleen, and in their brightness she came face to face with a row of paintings,

five of them, done in water-colours on plain rectangles
of paper and pegged on a piece of thin cord to dry. They
were semi-abstract landscapes and seascapes, two of
them containing human figures, done with a violence
and raw power that defied the genteel medium of water-
colour. Three of them were unfinished at the edges, with
brush strokes fading into the white of the paper as if the
artist had not the patience to fill an arbitrary space once
the main idea had been expressed. What the paintings
said to Prunella about the artist's love-hate relationship
with those boulders, headlands, fishing shacks and
stretches of shingle came through with such force and
clarity that she felt sure there was a true talent at work
here.

Upstairs, she didn't wait for Kathleen's comment
about her dress. 'Did you do those painting downstairs,
Katie?'

'Paintings?'

'Come and look.'

'Your dress is fine by the way, and gorgeous,'
Kathleen said.

'Is it? Thanks.' Prunella's reply was absent-minded.
'See, these!'

They both stood and looked at the paintings in silence,
and Kathleen reached up and touched one gently. The
paper crackled stiffly. 'Conlan said he'd been fiddling
with my water-colours—I left them here the other day—
and he hoped I didn't mind,' she whispered. 'I thought
he meant he'd been doodling some things to amuse the
kids. Is it just because he's my brother, or——?'

'No, I think they're wonderful too.' There was something raw and untrained about them, of course, but
talent and expression shone through strongly.

'I had no idea. No idea, at all.'

'Well, you've only just discovered your own talent,'
Prunella said.

'Did Conlan know before now that he could do this? No! I don't think he did. I think this is completely new for him.' Kathleen was half speaking to herself. 'If it makes as much difference to his life as it's making to mine. . .'

'Be careful, Katie. This is only a start. . .' Prunella knew, as Kathleen did not fully know, how much violence there was in Conlan Donovan's feelings. Rourke had told his sister a much watered-down version of the fight, and most hospital people thought that his bruises, still dramatically purple, were the result of a fall on a frosty path.

'Yes.' The dark-haired girl flapped her hands agitatedly as she turned away from the paintings. 'All right. But I know what I'm going to give him for Christmas— some paints of his own, and in the meantime I won't bother to take mine home again.'

The discovery created a mood of excitement in both of them, and when Prunella went into the girls' room and put on her make-up there in front of the mirror— much to Julia's interest and delight—she found that her cheeks didn't need rouge and her eyes were unusually alive within their landscape of subtly blended eyeshadow and glossy mascara.

Finlay noticed it too, and gave her what he clearly intended as a compliment—a caressing pat on the behind—as they left the house. There were seven people to squeeze into the spacious car, since four of Conlan's older children had arrived home from school and work in time to get ready and beg a ride. The vehicle was a black and silver Cadillac, and if this had sounded glamorous to Prunella the reality of its advanced years soon disillusioned her.

'Prunella in front with me,' Finlay decreed. 'And Mindy beside her. Katie and you others in the back. Tom, Ted, Lisa, no arguments!'

It was Prunella who wanted to argue. She was beginning to dislike Finlay, although she could see that Katie, to whom he was no threat, was fond of him in a cynical, amused sort of way. But to Prunella his flirting *was* a threat, because she didn't enjoy it and had to fend it off each time in a way that was firm without being rude.

I don't know how I could ever have thought he looked and sounded like Rourke, she found herself thinking—perhaps unwisely—and now there was only fourteen-year-old Mindy in front with her to act as chaperon, while Katie, who might have deterred Finlay a little, was squashed into one corner of the back seat by the boys, aged eighteen and nineteen, and sixteen-year-old Lisa.

'I was hoping Con would get home before we left,' Kathleen murmured, clearly still absorbed in the revelation of the paintings and in no state to distract her older brother from his wandering fingers. Unfortunately the car was an automatic and didn't require any changing of gears which might have kept his right hand busy.

'When are you going back to New York?' Prunella questioned firmly while she squeezed as close to quiet, redhaired Mindy as she decently could.

'Perhaps I'm not.'

'Aren't you wasting your time a bit, though, just hanging round here?'

'I've done a few odd jobs around Mum's house. Fixing leaking taps, and so forth,' he replied lightly. 'But wasting my time is what I do best.'

'So it seems,' Prunella said crisply, adding as she removed a hand very pointedly from her knee, 'You're certainly wasting it now.'

'I'll wait till later, in that case,' he grinned, unrepentant.

She sensed that his outrageous behaviour would be thoroughly toned down if she were visibly attached to someone else, and for a moment a painful, hopeless picture flashed across her inner vision of herself and Rourke side by side at family gatherings, arriving and leaving together, just the two of them, with a shared collection of jokes and understandings that Finlay and everyone else were quite shut out of.

What a stupid way to think! Angry with herself, she drew her blue wool coat more closely round her knees and wondered if she should have brought gloves. It was nearly the end of October and there was a change on the way. Some people were even talking about snow.

Still, I'll only be out of doors between the car and the house, she decided, and began to plot strategies for beating Finlay from the car to the front door and then losing herself at once in the crowd.

The momentum of the party was already building when they arrived, and, with a swish of her rustling silk dress and its attached tulle petticoat beneath, Prunella succeeded in leaving her coat on a rack in the hallway and threading between several hospital people to arrive at the drinks table with no Finlay Donovan in tow.

Rourke Donovan *was* there, however. Her dress brushed his trouser-clad legs and he had to juggle a newly filled wine glass to stop it from spilling on the black velvet of her bodice. 'Prunella!'

'Sorry, I. . .'

'Not your fault. I should have remembered that everyone in Newfoundland arrives early and stays late. I'd envisaged overlapping relays, and the house isn't big enough for everyone at once. What can I get you?'

'Nothing just yet. I. . . I brought you this.' She held the gift out to him, embarrassed. It seemed that most people had simply brought wine or food.

'Hey! What's this? I hope you haven't——'

'It's nothing.'

'Come into the kitchen.' He took the wrapped gift in

one hand and her wrist in the other and pulled her through the open door. Conlan's brood from Finlay's car were in there, raiding the fridge for a premature taste of supper, but Rourke ignored them as he pulled the red and white striped paper from the earthenware utensil jar Prunella had bought.

'I told you it was nothing,' she said as he held it up.

'What? Did you think I was expecting Orrefors crystal? I needed one of these.' He gestured to the catering-sized mayonnaise jar, label still intact, where wooden spoons, soup ladle and other items were currently stored. '*Now* can I get you a drink?'

'I'd love one, but very small, since I'm on home call.' She smiled up at him, and then wished she hadn't, because he put an arm around her shoulder and gave her a protective squeeze as if he was still worried, as an observant host, that she felt awkward and out of place.

It seemed as if his thoughts had been following the same train, because he took his arm away, poured her a half-glass of crisply chilled white wine and then said, 'Remember the first time you came here?'

'Of course.'

'It's about four months ago, I suppose. Perhaps four and a half, but it seems longer, doesn't it?'

'Perhaps,' she agreed cautiously, wishing that the crowd of people—many of them from the hospital—wasn't forcing them to stand so close to one another, and that the rising noise level didn't force him to bend towards her in order to be heard. 'Why do you say that?' she added.

'Because I think we've both changed,' he answered at once. 'You've become far less wary of people, for one thing.'

'That's true, I think,' she admitted. 'And yourself?'

'Me? Oh, I've realised a few things, and learnt something very important.'

There was a pause in which the way he gazed down at her was so disconcerting that she took refuge in speech again. 'Are you going to tell me what it is?'

He straightened away from her and now his eyes were very thoughtful. 'Shall I?' he mused aloud. 'No, not like this. I'm still not sure yet. . .quite what it means.'

'All right, then,' she laughed, trying to make light of what he was saying, although there was an undercurrent to it that she sensed was very serious.

Suddenly she thought of Meg Slade. According to Kathleen, Rourke had still said nothing about his intentions and plans for the future. 'And no one else has heard from her. Still. . .she's been moving into a new apartment. She must be very busy,' Kathleen concluded.

But Rourke was speaking again. 'Prunella, any other woman in the world would have begged me to tell her after an opening like that!'

'I can't help it,' she laughed. 'Tell me, if you want.'

'You're exasperating!'

'I'm trying to respect your privacy,' she said lightly, letting a rather wicked smile play on her lips, although she meant what she was saying. 'If it's important I'm not going to pry. I wouldn't want anyone to pry into my deeper realisations before I was ready to share them. When I *was* ready I'd hope there was someone waiting to listen.'

Incredibly she was actually enjoying this talk with him, and, though a part of her warned that this pleasure would only bring an even colder aftermath tomorrow when the party atmosphere was over, for now she did not want it to end.

It did, though, all too soon. Rourke had just begun an equally bantering and at the same time equally serious reply to her last words when Finlay suddenly materialised between them.

'Hello, brother!' He put an arm heavily around

Rourke's shoulders and gave them a rough squeeze. 'The place looks great,' he said. 'Tell me, though, was it really worth all that effort? You've been at it for, what, eight months, haven't you?'

'More,' Rourke answered easily. 'You forget that I had the foundations laid last autumn and did a lot of planning and ordering of supplies over winter.'

'So, answer my question. Was it worth it?'

'Yes.'

Finlay looked a little annoyed at the simple answer and turned to Prunella, laying a hand confidentially on her shoulder. 'What do you think, Nella? Oh, but perhaps you haven't looked the place over yet. Come on, let's take a tour.'

He pulled her through the crowd before she had the chance to protest, and she couldn't even look back to signal a mute apology to Rourke for her abrupt departure. She hated the fact that Finlay had called her Nella, too. It wasn't a shortening of her name that she liked or encouraged—no one else used it, and it implied a closeness between them that did not exist at all.

'Aha! The master bedroom!' Finlay said. He had almost dragged her down the corridor, and she intended to escape as soon as possible and retrace those steps, but for the moment he still had a firm yet caressing arm around her waist. 'What do you think of Rourke's taste in sheets?'

'Very nice.' She certainly wasn't going to tell him that she had slept between these sheets, with their Navajo-inspired pattern in warm earth tones. She suppressed a shudder as she thought of why she had been there—that icy near-drowning out in the dark water.

'And what do you think, Finlay?' came Rourke's voice smoothly behind them.

Finlay turned, startled into a laugh. 'Oh, I agree with Nell.'

'Prunella, Alan is trying to remember a detail about some surgery he did back in July,' Rourke said. 'He can't remember if you were scrubbing that day, but if you were. . .'

'I'll see if I can help,' she came in quickly, thankful to have a plausible exit line. Had Rourke really only come to relay Alan's message, though?

She didn't see him for the next few hours. Hot food was served, as a number of people had brought a quiche or a casserole as their house-warming contribution, and Prunella talked with several people she knew from the hospital, as well as most of the Donovans. It was when the hot supper was almost over that she found herself next to Rourke's mother.

'It's a lovely place he's made for himself, now, isn't it?' she said in her quiet way, and Prunella nodded.

'It suits him, I think,' she said. 'It means he can choose when to be with people and when to be alone.'

'It's too big for one person, though,' the grey-haired woman frowned. Her face was as wrinkled as old wrapping paper. Katie had told Prunella that she was seventy-two, and in many ways she looked older. 'And with the way he's got it ready for adding another bedroom, like. . .Pat Slade says that Meg won't ever come back here to live, so I wonder if Rourke has wasted his time with the building. You know, most people don't bother to build with stone around here. . .'

'Yes, it's a very permanent sort of thing, stone, isn't it?' Prunella agreed. 'I'm sure Meg will change her mind for Rourke's sake.'

'I'm not so sure,' the old lady said. 'Maybe she won't. And maybe that'll be the best thing that could happen for him.'

Her daughter-in-law Daphne came to bring her a cup of tea at that moment, so their conversation was at an end before Prunella could find out more clearly what

Mrs Donovan meant by that last thing. It was ambiguous, to say the least. Daphne greeted Prunella cheerily and would have embarked on a chat, but the latter slipped quickly away as soon as she had said hello. If Daphne was here then Conlan must be at home looking after Julia, Peter and the other three younger Donovans. The gulf between him and Rourke was such an exclusive thing, it seemed, that it didn't even extend to Daphne, who got on with Rourke very well.

How sad and futile it all is, Prunella thought, her spirits low suddenly. The house began to seem too crowded and noisy, and there were several smokers, filling the air with fumes that began to sting her eyes. Finding herself in the hallway, she decided to slip out quickly for a freshening breath of the cold night air.

Outside, she found a white fairyland. Over the last few hours snow had come. Late arrivals had mentioned it, but she hadn't taken the fact in. It had stopped falling temporarily now, and parts of the sky had opened up to become clear and star-filled again. Earlier, though, it must have been coming down heavily, because there was a frosting of two inches all over the ground.

As she watched, the moon escaped from behind a torn cloud and lit the landscape with silver. Waves came in to shore in long, fluted curls and splashed up against rocks and shingle to make frothing shapes of almost fluorescent white. In her light dress, she was immediately cold, but there was no wind and she found the chill almost exhilarating after the overheated crowding of the house. Hugging her arms around herself, she stood there drinking it in, almost not wanting to breathe in case the crystal-clear moment was shattered.

Then Rourke's voice came quietly behind her. 'You'll need this.'

She felt her wool coat, warm from the house, come to rest on her shoulders. She turned her head to thank him and found that his arms had stayed with the coat and were wrapping around her and his cheek was pressing against hers. For a long time they simply stood there in silence, watching the silver-white landscape, and she knew that he was as reluctant as she was to disturb it with words.

A part of her knew that this shouldn't be happening, that she should be as squeamish and reluctant about Rourke's arms as she was about his brother Finlay's, but in fact her feelings were utterly different. When he began to caress her and then turned her into his arms and nuzzled his lips against her hair, travelling with teasing kisses to her neck and then her jaw, cheeks and lips, her response was total, with no thought of the past or the future.

He tasted very slightly of coffee and chocolate and he smelled of aftershave and fresh sea salt. No, it was the sea itself she was smelling, as well as the fresh purity of snow in the air, and it seemed to lend a purity to this time with him so that she didn't even stop to wonder if they were being observed. As his hands moved to find and caress the female curves of her slender figure her own fingers kneaded the plaited muscles of his back and then came down to his hard hips, holding on to them as if for support.

It was Rourke who spoke first. 'Someone could come out of that door any minute, or decide to open the curtains. . .'

It was like a dousing of cold water, and she pulled away from him immediately. 'Oh!'

'I'm sorry, I didn't mean to be so abrupt.'

'No, it's. . . I hadn't thought of it, that's all.'

'Should I take that as a compliment?' he drawled.

She shook her head quickly, feeling her hair brush her cheeks in a light, frosty cloud. 'Don't play games, Rourke.'

Before he could respond the door did open, making both of them start guiltily, and when Prunella saw Finlay standing there, a rather fox-like grin making glinting slits of his green eyes, she knew she had started to blush.

'Sorry, you two,' he said. 'But it's warmer inside, you know.'

'Not necessarily,' Rourke growled.

'Really? That can only mean——'

'Get to the point, Fin, if there is one.'

'There is. It's the phone. Someone from the hospital.'

'A call-out?'

'I don't know. Daphne answered it.'

But Rourke hadn't waited for this reponse. Pushing past Finlay in the open doorway, he left Prunella alone in the snow, her feet in their black court shoes rapidly going numb. Finlay looked down at them. 'Hadn't you better come in?'

'Yes—I'm on call too. If it *is* something. . .'

She did not notice Finlay's wicked grin drop away, and was already trying to adjust to the fact that she and Rourke might be in surgery soon. The room was so crowded now that it was hard to push through to the kitchen, where the telephone was, and by the time she reached Rourke's side he had replaced the receiver.

'Anything to collect besides that coat?' he asked at once.

'No. I'm coming, then?'

'Yes. Where's Fin?'

'Right here,' came the voice that was sometimes like Rourke's and sometimes very different.

'I want you to find Katie and drive her to Conlan's.'

'What?'

'And tell Deirdre she's going to have Daphne. . .' Rourke pulled his brother firmly by the shoulder as he spoke, and they moved out of Prunella's hearing. Rourke had his back to her now, but over his powerful shoulder

she could see Finlay's face, and as he listened to his
brother the colour and slightly mocking good humour
drained out of it, leaving it stark and white. 'Come on,
Prue,' Rourke said.

He did not stay to observe the dramatic effect his
words had had on Finlay, and he pushed Prunella in
front of him as if he were a snow-plough and she its
blade, parting the loud clusters of people like heavy
drifts.

'Isn't there anyone else from here who——?'

'No.' He anticipated her question. 'Steve Wright was
on hospital call as Resident. Joel Nathan's there already,
finishing off an emergency C section. Don't know who'll
be circulating. Mr Scioto had a night off and I invited
him here, but he hasn't turned up. At home reading
medical textbooks, probably.' They were walking to the
Land Rover, their feet crunching in a rapid rhythm on
the snow. It was losing its feathery quality now that the
sky was clearer, and was becoming crisp and crusty,
although it looked as if more cloud and snow were on
their way. Rourke went on, 'Ignoring my efforts as a
tempter and sticking to his studently duty, our Joe.
There have been many occasions when I've done the
same.'

'Rourke,' she cut in desperately, 'you're rambling and
your jaw is like a vice. I saw Finlay's face, too, when you
were talking to him.'

They reached the vehicle, which was parked in the
garage that was as yet without a roof. Rourke threw
back the tarpaulin that had protected the windscreen
from snow and climbed into the driver's seat before he
answered. Sliding in beside him on the cold vinyl as
quickly as she could, Prunella found that her heart was
thudding apprehensively.

'It's Conlan,' Rourke said. 'There's been an accident.'

CHAPTER TEN

'A CAR accident?' Prunella said after a blurted exclamation and several moments of shocked silence. Then, 'But I thought he was at home, minding the children.'

'He was,' replied Rourke. 'They found a sticky red substance splashed on him and on the car, apparently. Finally worked out it was cough syrup. He must have gone out to get some.'

'Yes, Julia was complaining of a cough earlier this afternoon,' Prunella said slowly. 'She said it hurt her incision.'

'You've been there today?'

'Yes,' she nodded, then felt compelled to add, 'Conlan hadn't got home when Finlay picked the rest of us up.' Absurd to be afraid that Rourke might construe her friendliness with Conlan's family as disloyalty to himself, when there was this emergency at hand. She asked, 'How bad is it?'

'He's conscious, and has spoken, but internal organ damage is strongly indicated. . .' He sighed. 'We'll do an exploratory laparotomy and proceed from there.'

He said nothing further, and Prunella was silent too. He had to be thinking, as she was, that there was a chance they wouldn't be doing any surgery at all tonight. What would happen if Conlan simply refused point-blank to be treated by his brother? Dr Robert Innes, the hospital's director, had come up through the ranks of general surgery, but he now confined himself to major vascular cases. Blair Thompson, surgeon-in-chief at Curtis Hospital, could have done the operation, but he was away at an important two-day meeting in St John's.

Conlan Donovan would not be thinking along these lines, however. His rejection would be purely emotional.

Prunella remembered the paintings she and Kathleen had discovered that afternoon. 'He borrowed Katie's paints.'

'What?' Rourke frowned and spoke sharply.

'Conlan has been using Katie's water-colours to do some paintings of his own,' she explained more lucidly. Rourke's irritable response was quite understandable, given the way her initial remark had come out of the blue. 'I don't know much about art, as the saying goes, but to me they looked wonderful.'

'Why are you telling me this?'

He didn't look at her. The crusty film of snow on the road demanded all his attention, and she wondered if she should have guarded her tongue more carefully until a better time. She said hesitantly, 'I wondered if it might help him somehow. A means of self-expression. . .'

'You think water-colours are going to be the magic cure for two members of the Donovan family?' he questioned on a jeering note.

Suddenly she was angry. 'If you put it like that of course it sounds idiotic,' she snapped. 'But are you going to deny what a real change there's been in Kathleen over these past weeks?'

'No, I wouldn't deny that,' he answered slowly.

She waited for a moment, but he didn't say anything further, so she went on impatiently, 'It just seems to me that perhaps *you* are actually irrelevant to Conlan's problems. You've been the scapegoat for his frustration all these years, but the real problem is that he is a man of intelligence and ability who had never had a chance to fulfil it. He'd be just as angry at life if you were a. . .a. . .petrol-pump attendant, and if life has something for him after all. . .this painting thing, perhaps, since artistic talent seems to run in the family. . .Has anyone ever tried to teach him to read and write?'

'Of course,' Rourke said. 'Fiona did. It didn't work. He had too little confidence, too little patience, got too frustrated.'

'But if he's found out that he can paint it might give him the confidence and patience to tackle reading again. Or perhaps reading and writing won't be important if he has this other way to express himself.'

'Psychological jargon, Prunella.'

She was too angry to reply. He was simply blocking out her words, refusing to admit that there might be so much as a kernel of truth or hope in them. They were on the outskirts of town now and she could see the hospital ahead, its contours softened by snow. It was hard to believe, now, that Rourke had kissed her once again tonight. It kept happening, although clearly he didn't want it to. Was St Anthony too small for both of them?

But Rourke was speaking again. 'You may be right about one thing, though. . .'

'Thanks!'

He ignored her sarcasm. 'His bitterness against me. Perhaps it *is* a side-issue. No one's ever suggested that before. The family treats us both as if we've just never got over a bad pillow fight at the age of ten—Rourke and Conlan don't speak to each other. Silly! Awful! And it's got worse and worse over the years. But nothing can be done about it.'

'Sometimes you need a stranger to see these things with a fresh perspective,' she said, forgiving him a little.

He pulled into the car park and stopped the car. 'A stranger?' he repeated, giving her a long, odd look. 'Yes, perhaps it does take that. A stranger who somehow gets close.'

There was a moment of silence, then both of them stepped quickly from the car and into the cold air. There was no time to waste now on discussions of psychology. It was physiology that was all-important.

It was still less than half an hour since the accident had occurred. In the intervening time an IV had been put up and a trochar tapped into Conlan's abdomen to test for frank bleeding. Now, as soon as Rourke and Prunella were ready, the exploratory laparotomy would commence.

Prunella never got used to the sudden change of atmosphere that happened when she came in on call at night—the white lights, the sense of urgency, the need for perfect focus and alertness, and tonight she felt especially on edge. Conlan was waiting to be wheeled into Theatre, weak but still conscious. He was very pale and his stomach was distended in a way that pointed fairly conclusively to the organ damage Rourke had spoken about. He saw Rourke straight away.

'I thought it would be you,' he said, and there was twenty years' worth of bitterness in his tone, but at the same time an acceptance that had not been present the other day during their violent encounter in the hospital rotunda.

He closed his eyes and said nothing more, and Prunella thought, It's going to be all right. I don't believe it! It's going to be all right!

Instinctively she looked at Rourke, and found that he had one hand pressed to his eyes as if to massage away a sharp pain lying behind them. Suppressing a longing to press her own fingers soothingly against his temples, she went to the wash-room to scrub, the image of his strained yet thankful face still before her mind's eye.

It was stupid to get angry with him in the car, she realised. He was so tense that he had to express it in sniping and belligerence. And now perhaps his relief at Conlan's reaction was in danger of overwhelming him.

If only he wanted me, needed me, so that I could touch him now!

When had her feelings for him become love? Impossible to say. It had been a gradual process of change from the first sparkle of interest—as much, then, perhaps out of loneliness as for any other reason—passing through the brief, heady glow of his first kiss to arrive at a deep, stirring feeling that expressed itself sometimes as sensuosness, as anger, as friendship, or, now, as a painful yearning to help him in any way she could. When he entered the wash-room she couldn't even find a response to his brief question, 'Ready?' and so they prepared themselves for surgery in utter silence. . .

Prunella's shoulder ached as she held a retractor, and there was an itch on her nose that she longed to scratch. The hot lights made her eyes feel tired and strained, but she knew that it was the emotions of the night far more than the actual conditions of surgery that were responsible for how she felt—Rourke's kiss, Finlay's interruption, Conlan's accident. She couldn't think about the first two things now, but they were certainly colouring her response to the third. Carefully she let out a sigh and willed herself to relax and concentrate at the same time.

'Yes, look at that spleen,' Rourke was saying, not betraying by anything in his manner that this was his estranged older brother. 'It's going to have to go. Too messy to repair, and he can live very well without it.'

The injuries had been obvious as soon as they had opened up the abdomen. Rourke had warned the anaesthetist to expect a sudden increase in hypertension as the leaking blood escaped, and now that the area was drier he was examining the damage.

'There seems to be a laceration in the liver, too,' the resident, Steve Wright, said.

'Yes, we'll sew that over. It doesn't look too bad. He was very lucky. An inch or two to the right, or a mile or two faster. . .'

Rourke did the major work of removing the spleen, ligating the vessels that led to and from it, and sewing up the lacerated liver; then he stepped back wearily and said, 'I'm scrubbing out. Dr Wright, take over, will you? It's straightforward from now on.'

There was a degree of relief and satisfaction in his tone that Prunella knew was out of the ordinary. So he *had* been on edge! No one would have guessed at the time. He stayed in the background for a little longer, then left. Prunella, though, absorbed in her job, did not even have time to notice him go.

'Conlan wants you to go and see him,' Kathleen said, standing in Prunella's open doorway the next afternoon.

'Oh, yes, I was planning to,' Prunella answered easily. 'Come in, Katie, don't stand on the doorstep. I'll make tea. . .But I thought I'd give him a couple more days to recover, then. . .'

'No, I mean he wants you to go now,' Kathleen explained. 'I'm just the messenger. I haven't really come to visit. I'm on my way to the library to check on some whale facts. . .'

'Oh, all right.' Prunella was disappointed. Having spent the day on trivial matters such as laundry and letter-writing, she was ready to welcome a break and a chat. Since tomorrow she was on call for Medevac, this might be her only chance for socialising this weekend.

Kathleen saw that her friend was somewhat taken aback, and reached out to touch her arm briefly. 'Prue, I think he's got something to say. Wants to thank you, probably. He told the others—Daphne's there with two of the kids, and Alison popped in too—that they'd have to leave when you got there.'

'He needn't make a big thing of thanking me,' Prunella said. 'I was only——'

'Doing your job,' Kathleen finished sarcastically. 'Don't give me that! You're much more important than that, and you know it!'

'I'll have to change. . .'

'Visiting hour is over in fifteen minutes.'

'Staff perks, don't forget. They wouldn't throw me out unless they really had to.'

'I must dash, too, or the library will be closed before I've got anything done.'

Kathleen hurried away, leaving Prunella to contemplate her wardrobe quickly. Most of her clothes were still in the drier, and she wore only her Lycra work-out tights and a baggy sweater. It would have to be the purple jersey-knit dress, which was rapidly acquiring the status of an old stand-by. In five minutes she was hurrying across to the hospital building, wrapped hastily in her blue coat as it was cold and windy today, with more snow threatening in the grey sky.

Conlan smiled weakly at her as she entered. He was alone, and Eileen, who worked on this ward, said quietly as she came past, 'We sent his family home. He's too tired, as you can see, and in pain, although he's being very good about that. Don't spend too long.'

'I won't,' Prunella murmured in reply. She prepared some soothing phrases for Conlan, but they were unnecessary.

'Didn't call you in just for a talk,' he said, speaking with an effort. 'I need you to go and see Rourke. You'll know what to say. Don't make me put it into exact words for you. I. . . I can't face him myself yet, to thank him, but I will. One day. I can't send someone in the family, either. It needs to be someone like you, a stranger. . .and a friend at the same time.'

'Why don't you. . .' she trailed off—'write him a

letter?' was what she had started to say '. . .wait until you're stronger to talk about this?' was the lame ending she came up with. Like most people, she took reading and writing for granted, and it was hard to imagine how someone's life must be without those abilities.

'I don't want to wait,' Conlan said. 'I'll change my mind—I know it. This isn't some sunny miracle of forgiveness. It's just the first step, and I know I'll take ten backward paces after this.' He was tiring himself visibly, but Prunella felt powerless to stop the flow of words, just as she had been the other day in the rotunda. 'I feel so lucky and happy to be alive. . .' His hand trembled as he brought it to his face and pressed it briefly over his eyes. He *was* lucky to be alive, Prunella knew. Those injuries could easily have been so much worse. The spleen was one of the few organs that could simply be removed once it was damaged. 'But that won't last. We all take life so much for granted, don't we?'

'Yes, that's true,' Prunella murmured, noticing the way his turn of phrase had echoed her own thought.

'So tell me you'll go and see him now. I need to know you're going and I need you to give him this.'

He tried to reach out to the small bedside table next to him, but it was too awkward a movement and he was too tired. Prunella darted forward. 'This?' There was a plain manila envelope there, quite large, containing what felt like a single sheet of rather stiff paper.

'Yes. You've got it? Good. And you'll go.' His eyes closed at once, and Prunella could see that, in his need, he was unconcerned that she might have reasons for not doing as he asked. *Did* she have reasons? Only one. She was in love with Rourke and wanted to avoid him, particularly in emotion-fraught encounters such as this one had the potential to be. It was scarcely something she could tell Conlan about, though, and in the face of his need it was a reason she had to ignore.

'Yes, Con,' she said softly after nearly a minute of silence. 'I'll go.'

He didn't respond and, fearing that he might have fallen asleep and not heard, she reached out and touched the hardened hand that lay on the white hospital sheet. He opened his eyes, smiled drowsily and said, 'Thank you,' then the eyes closed again, and this time she knew that he slept.

It wasn't until she was outside the building that the crucial fact occurred to her—she had no car to get to Rourke's.

I can't let that stop me, she thought, and the alternatives began to present themselves—walking, hitch-hiking, phoning Rourke and asking him to meet her in her room. None of these appealed, although she realised it would be sensible to telephone first to make sure he was home.

She was standing in the car park as she thought, and it was by no means warm. The place was quiet now, too, since visiting hour was over. Then a long, large machine cruised into the driveway, its engine vibrating with a low, hollow throb that didn't sound too healthy. It was Finlay Donovan's Cadillac, and his eyes lit up when he emerged from it and saw Prunella standing there.

'I'm too late, aren't I? Visiting hour is over,' he said. 'Typical!' He seemed almost to relish his own failure to heed such conventions as visiting hours. 'Will they let me in?'

'No, and they might not have even if it had still been visiting hour,' she said. 'He's had a few people through, and he's very tired.'

'Oh, you've seen him, then.'

'Yes, just for ten minutes.' She had decided straight away that she wouldn't mention the special reason for her visit, but. . .that ridiculous black and silver car.

Could she ask to borrow it? Would she succeed in driving it if she did? 'Finlay . . .are you going on anywhere else?'

'No. . .or, at least, a drink was on the agenda. Would you——?'

'Something rather urgent has come up,' she said. 'I can't explain. If I dropped you at the hotel—or any-where—and brought the car back afterwards, could I borrow it for an hour?' An hour was surely enough time.

'A mysterious quest, eh? Surely! Have it for two, as long as you join me at the hotel once you've finished.'

'Of course.' She manufactured far more pleasure than she felt. 'A drink would be nice.'

'Hmmm.' He narrowed his eyes shrewdly. 'This errand must be important if you're prepared to go that far.'

She blushed, and realised for the first time that he knew exactly how she felt about him and was deliber-ately teasing her with his apparent ardour. 'Your trouble is that you haven't got enough to do, Finlay!' she snapped at him bluntly, and he grinned.

'I know. I'm off to Montreal next week.'

'Not New York?'

'New York didn't want me.' Behind the flippant response Prunella saw a grain of more sombre feeling. She was learning a lot about Finlay Donovan this afternoon.

'I'm sorry, Fin,' she said sincerely.

'I'm not.' And it was back to the familiar manner.

'Well, wherever you go,' she said mischievously now, 'Glenda will miss you.'

'Glen——?' He broke off as light dawned, then grinned. 'Yes, I expect she will.'

They both laughed, then he shivered as a sudden gust of cold wind caught at their clothing. He said, 'He's a lucky man, Prunella Murdoch.'

'Who?'

'The man who's going to get you. I wonder if I know who it is. . .'

'I very much doubt it,' she made herself return. 'I haven't met him yet.'

'I wonder. . .'

If you're thinking of your brother Rourke, she wanted to say, then you're way off course. But before she could say anything he had touched his lips to her cheek in a light, dry kiss, and dropped the car keys into her hand. 'I'll walk to the hotel. Pick me up there when you're ready and we'll have that drink.'

He turned on his heel and strode off in the opposite direction with such an air of finality that he was a hundred yards away before she realised that she hadn't asked him how to drive the car. It was an automatic, she remembered, but beyond that. . .

Half an hour later the powerful old engine died as she turned off the ignition outside Rourke's solitary cottage. Her phone call to him had been brief, and his manner guardedly cheerful. 'Any hints as to what it's about?'

'None, I'm afraid,' she had said, trying to sound light in tone.

'Then I'll have to occupy my mind in speculations while I'm cleaning fish.'

'You were out today?'

'Just for an hour this morning. I've got the dinghy out here now. But it got too rough, so the catch wasn't impressive.'

'Well. . .see you in a while.'

'Yes. 'Bye.'

He was waiting for her at the opened outer door and came forward as she got out of the car. 'That's Finlay's Cadillac.'

'Yes,' she nodded. 'I had no other way of getting out here.'

'I could easily have come in, if it was important.'

'It's all right.'

'Was it hard to drive?'

'Not really,' she lied, not wanting to admit that she had been gritting her teeth and wincing at every engine noise for the entire trip, which she had taken at twenty-five miles an hour.

'Well, this is a bitter wind,' he said, 'so come in.'

He took her elbow and steered her beside him. Risking a glance upwards, she saw that his bare head was being buffeted and that his eyes were narrowed against the sting of the air. Her own blue Paisley scarf provided good protection. He slid it from her hair, then slipped her coat from her shoulders and hung them both on an antique clothes-stand that looked just right here in the entrance hall.

Inside, a fire crackled in the grate and there was the fresh smell of hot, strong coffee. A pot and two fragile cups sat on the low table in front of the hearth, and he poured out the rich brown liquid straight away. There were shortbread biscuits on a plate as well.

'So what's this about?' he said as he handed her the steaming cup. 'Or do you make a habit of driving Finlay's car around the countryside for idle chats?'

There was an undercurrent to his words, and Prunella realised that he was reading far too much into the loan of the car. Foolishly she wanted to set him straight, but, after all, why did it matter if he thought she was newly involved with Finlay? It wouldn't change the status of their own non-relationship.

'Not a chat, Rourke,' she said, putting aside her own emotions for the sake of the more important task she had come to perform. 'Conlan sent me.'

'Con did?' His black frown reminded her of the first time she had heard him mention his brother's name. It would be ironic if last week's fight had made Rourke too bitter to forgive when at last Conlan was ready to make the first move. The bruise on Rourke's face was still a purple-grey shadow beneath his high, prominent cheek-bone, and there was a new pink scar, the shape of a cat's claw, just below the corner of his lip.

'Yes, he. . .' She stopped, unable to find words, then remembered the envelope she still held. 'He wanted to give you this.'

She did not know what the envelope contained, but intuition told her that it might say more than her words at first. He took it at once from her outstretched hand, opened the unsealed flap and, still standing in front of the fire, slid the sheet of paper out. Prunella could see from where she sat that it was one of Conlan's paintings, although she did not think it was one that had been hanging on the cord yesterday. Rourke looked at it for a long time in silence, then a shout of laughter escaped from deep within him. 'This is. . .amazing!'

'He's good, isn't he?'

'Not just that. This picture shows an event that happened nearly twenty-five years ago. He took me out fishing and I caught a cod nearly as big as I was. It was probably the closest he and I have ever been.' Something caught the light in the corner of his eye and she saw that it was a tear.

'Then you don't need me to tell you what he said to me.'

'Yes, I do.'

Carefully she told him of the scene, not holding back on Conlan's prediction that there were still many bitter, unforgiving moments to come. Rourke listened and nodded at it all. 'I'm glad he's not promising instant closeness. I wouldn't have believed it if he had.'

They thrashed the matter over for several more minutes, then Prunella realised that there was nothing left to say about it for the time being. 'I should go,' she said. 'I told Finlay I'd only be an hour.' It was too disturbing to see Rourke like this, with his guard down. It made her want to reach out to him in a way that was far too dangerous.

'Well, if Finlay calls, a woman must come running, I suppose,' Rourke said lightly.

'Don't be idiotic, Rourke,' she blurted crisply. 'It's not like that.'

'Isn't it?'

'No.'

'And yet you seem so involved with the Donovan family. Conlan asked you to bring this.' He touched the painting once again. 'Katie's so close to you. I'm starting to think there has to be a deeper reason.'

'Could it simply be that I like the Donovan family?' she returned.

'I don't know. Could it?'

'It's what has made me put down roots here in St Anthony.'

There was a stillness in the air now and she was aware of how closely he was watching her, although the room was growing dim in the late afternoon. She saw that the flames of the fire had died, too, to a bed of hot, bright coals, and rose to go and hold her hands out to them, needing a way to avoid meeting those eyes of his. But he caught at her wrists so that she had to stand and face him, and inevitably her gaze was drawn upwards to lock with his.

'Just that, Prue?' he said very softly, caressing her hands with his. 'Couldn't it be something to do with you and me?'

'I don't know,' she mimicked him. 'Could it?'

'If it were just up to me, yes, very much.' He drew her close to him and kissed her, his lips trying to coax words from her even as they stopped her from speaking. But she was still too wary of this. It had happened three times before and had left only hurt and uncertainty.

Feverishly she pulled away as his hands trailed hotly down her back. 'Rourke, don't do this. Does it mean something, or is it just loneliness because Meg is in Toronto? Don't pretend. Don't talk about friendship or keeping our distance, then break the bargain as soon as we're alone. I can't live with that.' Unseeingly she twisted the purple fabric of her dress in tense, clawed hands.

'I asked Meg to marry me two days before she left here,' Rourke said.

'Yes,' Prunella nodded, freezing. So it was to be another knife wound! 'Everyone's been saying——'

'Let me finish, Prunella Murdoch. She turned me down.'

'Ah! So this is on the re——'

Inexorably he went on speaking. 'I've never been so happy about anything in my life,' he said, and imprisoned her in a caressing hold that she could not escape. 'You see, I had it in my head that I had to marry a local girl if I wanted to stay in St Anthony. When she turned me down it told me in a flash what an idiot I was. I realised I was in love with you, but I still told myself that I wouldn't do anything about it because you'd want to go back to Scotland. That's when I told you that I just wanted to be friends. Even at that stage I was kidding myself that I could ride out what I felt. Then it became clear pretty quickly that I couldn't, and we made that ridiculous agreement about keeping our distance, but it's been such hell—when I've managed to stick to it——' He broke off to kiss her again. 'Seeing you last night at the party, hearing your perception about Conlan and myself. . . It finally clicked. No place, no roots, no commitment is more important than what I feel about you. I'll leave tomorrow if that's what you want.'

'But I *don't* want to,' she laughed, daring to believe in

his kiss at last. 'Not if you're in my life. I feel more at home here than I did in my tiny, arid world at home.' Briefly she talked about her family and the fact that it had no real niche for her.

'Then you'll stay, here in this house?'

'I love this house.'

'As my wife, Prue?' he whispered very softly.

'As your wife,' she answered, her lips nuzzling the words into his ear, and her eyes closed so that her other senses could drink him in more fully.

'It's ironic,' he said a long while later. 'I thought that only a local girl would understand this place, understand my family, but Meg wants to stay in Toronto, so my cold-blooded determination to make myself fall in love with the woman was flawed from start to finish.'

'Didn't it succeed even a tiny bit?' she asked wickedly.

'What do you mean, witch? I can see that glint in your green eyes.'

'Didn't you fall even a small bit in love with her?'

'Will this answer for me?'

His kiss went on for so long that it must have had a great deal to say in answer to her question. The coals popped in the grate and their two bodies were caressed by warmth as well as by each other. Outside, the wind gusted and wailed around the house, making it seem like the safest haven in the world.

I'm not straying from here, from his arms, Prunella thought, until—— She remembered Finlay's car. She had already stayed well beyond the promised hour. 'Rourke, this is too awful! I have to go and give Finlay back his wretched Cadillac!' she said, pressing her ear against Rourke's chest and listening to his heart beating. 'I promised I'd have a drink with him.'

'Really?' Rourke held her at arm's length and raised one craggy black eyebrow. 'We'd better get going, then.'

'We?'

'Darling Prue, if I don't follow behind you in the Land Rover, how will you get back here to my place afterwards?'

'Hm, yes, I didn't think of that,' she answered.

Then, as they clung to each other without making any attempt to depart, he whispered, 'On the other hand, perhaps I could phone Fin at the hotel and suggest that he really doesn't need his car until tomorrow. . .'

AUTHOR'S NOTE

ALTHOUGH the Charles S Curtis Memorial Hospital in St Anthony, Newfoundland, actually exists, and I have tried wherever possible to be accurate in my depiction of the hospital and the town, many changes have, of course, been made. My sincere thanks go to the staff at the hospital who assisted in my research, and to the Grenfell Museum for information relating to the early days of the town and its pioneering medical service. I must stress, however, that no contemporary character or event portrayed in this novel has any foundation in reality whatsoever.

-MEDICAL ♥ ROMANCE-

The books for enjoyment this month are:

MORE THAN TIME Caroline Anderson
LOVING QUEST Frances Crowne
CLOSER TO A STRANGER Lilian Darcy
DIAMONDS FROM DR DALY Angela Devine

♥　♥　♥　♥　♥

Treats in store!

Watch next month for the following absorbing stories:

THE CALL OF LOVE Jenny Ashe
A HEART UNTAMED Judith Worthy
WAITING GAME Laura MacDonald
THE WESSEX SUMMER Sarah Franklin